ISLAND STORIES

ISLAND STORIES

Photo Canva/design
Cover created by the author

ELEVEN STORIES COLLECTED

Juidson Campos

Original Title
Eleven Stories Collected
First edition

ISBN: 9798374953299

Canva cover art/Design
@juidson

To Darci de Souza Guimarães e Dário.
(In memoriam)

"Youth is the time to study wisdom; old age is the time to practice it."

JEAN JACQUES ROUSSEAU

— SUMMARY —

ISLAND STORIES

FIRST PART

THE GOALKEEPER'S NOSE

It was the day before the game. We trained a lot. I play on the left. Régis is the fourth defender. The team, Jequié Football Club, had just qualified for the quarterfinals, we were preparing for the first game; for now, it was only with teams from the region. Coach Walter Oliveira was already excited, but he was also worried. It happened to be the end of the year, so he would rather not see us partying until late at night. It was great. We understood the message, but not to the point of refusing Rita's invitation. She had just become 15 years old, so we went there, and came back with Luiz, our goalkeeper, before he decided to ruin the birthday girl's party just because she had recently left him. Well, that did not happen; or rather, he did not show up at all. It was for the best. Rita was happy. He would just be a pain in the ass, in which case we wouldn't have to see him wanting to stick his finger in the cake. We were satisfied. Maybe he was already at home, cooling off. The next day we would concentrate at the club, the game would be in the afternoon, by then he would be fine. Régis and I even left the party early. We took the way back, following the square.

Then, to our surprise, we saw our goalkeeper stretched out on the bench in the square, completely drunk.

“It's not posible.” I said, turning away from the suit, walking over to him.

"He stuck his face in the bar, he didn't show up there, I'm sure of it," said Régis, following behind.

Luiz was sleeping with his mouth open under the mercury light pole, with moths fluttering around the bulb.

“He looks bad.” I said, touching his face.

“I want to see tomorrow”, said Régis, already anticipating the loss.

“What's gotten into him?”

“Elbow pain,” replied Régis, suddenly laughing.

"We have to get him out of here; otherwise, he won't play tomorrow!"

“Walter will tell him to go fuck himself,” Régis continued, wryly.

I lifted his arm, searching for his wrist.

“Do you know where he lives?”

Régis pointed in the direction of Mount *Pitangueiras,* on the other side of the avenue, at the bend in the waterfront.

“Behind the white house,” Régis showed.

I let go of Luiz's arm to look.

“Where?”

“Up there, near the palm tree!”

“The green house?”

"Yeah."

"We'll get there, tomorrow!"

"Unlucky for *Balthazar*[1]."

I was undecided, not knowing what to do.

"Where's the shortcut?"

"On the curve", Régis pointed once more, this time in the direction of Flag Beach.

"Aw, those trees?"

"A staircase starts there."

I looked again at the goalkeeper passed out on the bench.

"Damn, Luiz", I yelled pissed off, "how did you go and stuff your face like that?"

I looked again toward the hill, calculating the distance, the effort.

"Not soft, what the hell, why did I have to come that way," I complained.

"With him like this, I believe one hour."

"Fuck it, he'll come up on his own!"

"I want to see."

I tried to force him to sit down by pulling on his arm.

"Leave me the fuck alone," grumbled the drunk.

"Luiz, wake up!" I shouted, pulling him harder.

"Fuck you," he cursed loudly, out of tune.

---

[1] In Portuguese, the word 'azar' (bad Luck) rhymes with Balthazar, a slang expression of the time.

"You're the one who should go asshole!"

Régis laughed.

I went around the bench to help lift him up on his back. His head would not stop standing. With Régis's help, we slung the poor person's arms over our shoulder, trying to steady him between us.

"I've never seen drinking like that before," I commented, panting.

"Not either," nodded Régis, regaining his breath.

"Luiz, wake up!" I shouted next to the idiot's ear.

The drunk's eyes quite opened, seeming to swirl in alcoholic delirium.

"Luiz, wake up!"

"Rita, my dear," he mumbled in a soft voice.

I become my face sideways. Unbearable breath.

"I'm not Rita, you dear son of a bitch!"

Régis laughed, debauched.

"Talk to him, Rita, he wants a kiss!"

"What's gotten into him, anyway?"

"They had a fight, that's what."

"Did they have to fight today?"

"She didn't say anything."

"I know, she's always keeping to herself."

Régis yawned looking at the moon. Luiz still had his arms over our shoulders; in fact, it was at that moment that we perform that we had to start walking with him between us, before he decided to move away and could continue sleeping outdoors. This decision immediately made sense due to the lack of a better option, as-time was running out, bringing the cold dawn. We left the square with him on our shoulders, bent under the dying weight as his legs dragged, sometimes braiding like a rag doll, sometimes staggering like a street drunk.

After crossing the avenue, already at the base of the stairs, with much effort, we had to sit on the first steps, still with him between us. Despite the sea breeze, sweat dripped from our faces, but the worst thing was that, sitting there, we knew that behind us was the long climb up the winding hill.

"How did that happen?" Asked Régis, wailing, panting.

"Idiot!"

"Rita had nothing to do?"

"This idiot is the one who didn't!"

The drunkard woke up nodding his head, and then wanted to play the romantic poet.

"My torn heart are tears shed, that in the dark of the cold night, under the dripping dew, the juice of my life flowed..."

"What did he say?" Régis wanted to know, dumbfounded, inattentive.

"I don't know, *he said he's ass in hand, it's dark, he's crying...* I don't remember anymore".

Régis let out a laugh.

"We'd better not waste any more time," said.

We lifted our friend in our arms and become to face the stairway, beginning our climb, systematically. Anyone passing by and seeing the ridiculous scene would surely be watching three drunkards lost at night.

"My broken heart is tears..."

"*Cachaça!*[2]" I shouted in his ear to stop him from continuing the despicable verse. "

"No, thank you," he replied, "but I'll have a vodka with lemon!"

I didn't have time to revile him, but suddenly, someone was coming down from upstairs. He was passing under the spotlight when we saw that it was an old man smoking a pipe.

"Isn't that his grandfather?"

"The staircase serves as access to the street upstairs, it could be anyone," Régis explained, also examining the old man slowly descending.

Our friend suddenly insisted on the step and looked at us in astonishment, one at a time, frowning until he vesgantly recognized us.

"What are you doing here?" He asked as he swayed his body like a hammock.

"We're taking you home." I replied sullenly.

"Where is the boy from my *caipirinha*[3]?"

---

[2] Sugar cane brandy produced in Brazil.

[3] Caipirinha is a Brazilian alcoholic drink made with *cachaça*, lime, sugar and ice.

"That's enough, Regis, let's go home now, you idiot."

"I want to talk to Rita!" He yelled pulling his arm from around my shoulders as Regis staggered forward, dragging Luiz with him.

"Let's fall backwards!" He screamed.

We fell. Moreover, we really fell because Luiz's body bent over and Régis went with him, dragging my body with him. Even the old man, who was coming down from above, took his pipe out of his mouth to observe the fall of many legs, arms, heads, and asses rolling back down the stairs. With the shock of the fall, the goalkeeper's nose leaked blood over his lips and neck. Régis skinned his elbow. It was worse with me. I had sprained my right foot, and I was leaning against the corner of the wall, full of rage and pain.

"I think Luiz has shattered his nose," Régis said startled, standing up, and looking closer.

"I bet he's breathing," I commented, groaning, segueing my foot in pain. I couldn't move it properly.

Régis approached me.

"Is it serious?"

"I think I twisted it."

"The one who won't like to hear that is Walter."

The old man approached us.

"What's going on around here, young people?"

"We're trying to get our friend home," said Régis, rearing up in front of the old man.

"He's drunk," I added.

"Just him?" Questioned the old man blowing cheap pipe smoke on us. I replied with a shake of my head.

"Looks like they dried up the still!"

"He dried it out," I restated, already annoyed.

"He's a drunk with a broken nose," Régis added, smiling.

The old man looked at him. He noticed blood clots on his face. He stared contemplatively for ten or more seconds, then came down the last few steps. Not only that, but he looked at us, and suddenly let out a laugh, become his back to us, coughing as he continued on his way to the bend in the sea. In silence, Régis and I continued to watch him walk away from us, and occasionally, he laughed, coughing.

The old man looked at him. He noticed blood clots on his face. He stared contemplatively for ten or more seconds, then came down the last few steps. Not only that, but he looked at us, and suddenly let out a laugh, become his back to us, coughing as he continued on his way to the bend in the sea. In silence, Régis and I continued to watch him walk away from us, and occasionally, he laughed, coughing.

I tried to stand up using to withstand on the sidewall. I placed my twisted foot on the floor, trying to stabilize it. The throbbing pain forced me to give up.

"Goodbye championship," I muttered desolately.

"Walter will go crazy."

"Fuck!"

Régis got up and went to Luiz again. He examined his nose. He crouched down to get a better look at it.

"It stopped bleeding" — he reported.

"Too bad, I wish it had flown into the asphalt, a truck would have crushed it for good," I lamented.

Luiz regained his senses, moved his arm, tried to lift his head unsuccessfully, but he lifted his hand to scratch his nose and felt something jelly-like on his fingers.

"What's that?"

"It's menstruation!" I shouted angrily.

"Menstruation," he babbled, placing his fingers near his eyes.

"Whose menstruation?"

"Rita's, who else's could it, be?"

"Rita's? What do you mean? " He continued puzzled, rubbing his fingers above his eyes, and then immediately stuck them in his mouth.

"It tastes like blood."

"Serious? It's not vodka?"

"Where is it? He wanted to know, trying uselessly to lift his head up.

Régis looked up the stairs, not caring what he said.

"How are we going to take him?"

"I said, let's leave him right here."

Suddenly, Régis looked at me the way he does when he is setting up a defensive play.

"I have an idea!" Finally. I braced myself. I knewshit was coming.

"I'll go to Flax's house and explain to his parents what happened!"

"What?"

"That's right, we found him in that state! What could if you do? Well, then someone will come down and soon everything will be sorted out! We will explain that we tried to climb with him and that it was no longer possible because you twisted your foot." He paused, certainly waiting for my approval; but, as I said nothing but stared, he decided to insist.

"You must be making fun of my face," I still replied.

"Why?"

"Because that's not an idea, that's the whole truth, you idiot!"

"Okay, I'm an idiot, but I'm going there!"

"Luiz's mom will be scared, I am not convinced that's a good idea," I observed, looking up.

"No way," he retorted, "they'll understand, after all, everyone ends up drinking over the top sometime!"

"Okay, God willing," I agreed, already shrugging my shoulders.

"I'll be right back."

Régis took the long stairway, disappearing in the bright reflections of the night-lights. I was silent, the breeze was blowing on the branches of the tall trees near the bend; when the rustling of the leaves ceased, I heard Luiz's breathing, snoring in a deep, drunken sleep. I saw the blood crystallize just below his nose; his lips, his teeth, were still bloody, giving that frightening impression that he had suffered a stroke. At that minute, I thought it would not be a very pleasant scene for whoever was going down.

As I watched him with my head now resting against the wall, I wondered what motivated our youth to drink in this way, at least to the point of losing their balance, and as if this were not enough thought about the increase in drug use throughout the region. This amazed me. Not only because I saw friends committing futile follies. The world was really changing too fast without giving us time or quiet to understand ourselves more lucidly. I could see this in the older people.

Suddenly, people began to descend. Footsteps and voices were blowing in the wind. The glare of the night was blinding me with the streetlights, preventing me from seeing them clearly; but as they approached the halfway point of the staircase, I could see their faces: two men were coming down, followed by a woman. Régis was in the front, still talking. He had a certain shy expression in his gestures as he tried to explain what had just happened to us; at the same time, I felt my heart beating faster. Maybe it was thinking that we had left it at that, what friends, Hein! They were getting closer and closer, when then the woman came forward to hug her son.

"Oh, Jesus Christ", she said with her hands to her mouth as she crouched down to finally saying in a crying voice:

"Little Louis, my beloved son, what have they done to you?"

Faintly, Louis mumbled something intelligible as he tried to fix his gaze on his mother's anguished face.

"Now all is lost, Mama," he said, tragically, *"now my heart is torn in tears shed, Mama!"*

"What happened, my dear..." She continued, examining her son's face in a choked voice, stroking him in tears as she noticed his nose bathed in blood.

"That won't help now, Lourdes, let's get him home first," one of the men said as he approached.

"He's right, Lourdes," said the other man, already holding him by the arm, saying with some effort as he tried to lift him up:

"What he needs is a cold bath, after a sugary coffee. He'll talk better tomorrow. "

"Not a cold bath at this hour, poor guy, he might catch a cold!"

His mother was surprised and distressed.

The two men withstand him on their shoulders. They had strength and good height, and were ready to start the climb with him entwined in the middle.

"Be careful, you might fall," Régis warned behind them, worried.

The drunk woke up again for a moment, become to look at one of them, still saying what he had just heard:

"You're absolutely right, now that's no good, already the earth *consumes the dripping dew.*"

"Take this handkerchief, little son, put it over your nose," the distressed mother said.

I had to hold back my laughter, my throat even hurt, I even forgot about my throbbing foot.

The climb was slow. We followed the completely vague path from a distance, watching them from the base of the stairs. I also noticed Régis' effort to hold back his laughter; he seemed afraid to look at me and ruin everything.

Finally, they disappeared behind the reflection of the lights, leaving us with a silence broken only slightly by the rustling of the leaves on the trees.

Finally, it was our turn. Régis helped me along the way back home. We also took our time as they did. I had to walk carefully, without touching my right foot to the ground. We walked a good distance like that, in limp silence. The street was silent too; only again and again, when, without saying a word, we suddenly burst into laughter just remembering the scene, imitating the voice of Luiz's mother, saying: poor little nose of my beloved son… imagine, cold bath, poor thing, he catches a cold!

Surely, the next day, we would be anxious to see our goalkeeper enter the club. Oh, we wouldn't forgive. We could already imagine, him showing up in the locker room with a swollen nose, and all of us saying:

"Poor litte thing".

RAFA'S BAR

We were at the bar when suddenly a formidable downpour came from the clouds. The sky, to put it simply, almost fell down as well. The rain was so heavy that, moments later, many sparrows also began to fall from the almond trees. They looked like little angels falling from the sky, all drenched by the sudden scourge. The sidewalk of the bar by the intersection of street Serrão and Peixoto de Carvalho, simply, without exaggeration, was full of sparrows. Moreover, all of them, terrified, struggled desperately, flapping their sodden wings as if trying to fly, but exhausted, they remained on the ground.

Rafa, aware of these instant storms in January and February, immediately began to provide plastic boxes from the backyard, where the bottle storage was; then he ordered us to pick up the birds from the sidewalk, before they were swept away by the current that descended like a rapid waterfall into the sewers.Well, that's what we did. We ran under the storm, each in possession of a box, and bravely braved the torrential rain that beat us like an icy whip on our bare backs. In a matter of minutes, our sweat was washed off as we rounded up a flock of sparrows on the ground. Several of them, however, were lost; we no longer saw them, not even across the street, such was the smoke from the water rising from the hot asphalt. In fact, we had never seen anything like it.

That same day, when everything seemed forgotten in the middle of the sunny afternoon, the sparrows began to stir in the bins. Ralph then decided to open the bins. They still looked frightened, so some of them, about five or six bolder ones, slowly jumped under the tables just above our feet, headed for the door, and quickly flew off into the sky. At this point, by the way, many people passing by were surprised. Currently, it was funny. We were standing in front, sitting on the steps outside the bar, excited by the various expressions of surprise that passersby were making in our direction and, of course, watching the birds fly out of the bar. We had to hide to laugh, it was fun, and then we laughed until we couldn't anymore.

Much more amusing was the reaction of old Maya. An old retired sailor from the old Navy. It was the height of mockery, the adjective *old*; this, to show that he was a survivor of the 18th century. Although we did not believe what was said about him, including that he had fought in the Battle of Riachuelo[4]. Furthermore, that he had served honorably on the same ship as Admiral Barroso[5], who we

[4] The War of the Triple Alliance (1864-1870), the biggest conflict in the history of South America,

[5] Military of the Brazilian Imperial Navy.

later learned had sunk five ships in Solano Lopez's fleet. We were amazed at their such creative ability to lie about the old man just because he was that old. Oh, but don't think it was just any old man, not old Maya .... Yes, well. He was already a little drunk when he entered the bar (he had the usual afternoon apéritif). He soon fixed his passion fruit liquor as he pulled up a chair to sit with the others; on this day, he seemed more animated than on other days. He explained about a nautical engine he had bought when he arrived in town; finally, as he had met Alencar on the way, he told him he had the engine, so the two of them went to the garage to close the big deal, and blah, blah, blah....

Yes, but it's good to remember. While he was explaining about the engine purchase, the sparrows kept jumping under the tables. Somehow, of course, Old Maya had even noticed, although he didn't seem to believe it. Oh, come on. A bird circling the bar was not a common thing to see there. The truth was, the birds' flight got louder and louder, even under his chair, so he decided to interrupt the engine business and get Ralph's attention by questioning him:

"Did you by any chance decide to change parishes?"

"What are you talking about, Maya?"

"Hell, what am I talking about, two little birds just jumped over my foot just now!"

Obviously, everyone looked at each other, concealing nothing unusual. Nobody had any intention of spoiling the opportune moment to provoke him even more, to the point that someone even warned him to stop drinking because he was raving about 'bird customers', that was the end of the matter!

"Oh, no, not that one!" He shouted, irritated.

"Are you going to say I'm the only one who can see these pimply birds?"

"Pimply birds? What pimps, Maya? " Asked another idiot at the table, become to the counter to ask Ralph not to serve passion fruit liqueur to the sailor, since he was hallucinating.

"That's right, all that's left is to say that we're the ones who are drunk, he's not!" Added another from the next table, with the cynicism of a theatrical actor.

The old sailor, hearing this, was dumbfounded. He was not convinced by the provocation thrown in the air. He ended up calling everyone a liar. Yes, he ended up reaffirming that he had seen two sparrows pass under his chair! A sight he couldn't be wrong about, just because he was an old man of almost a hundred years with an occasional sip of passion fruit rum!

Everyone laughs.

Confronted with this commotion, he finished by saying that he would agree that he was a little crazy. Not crazy with a card hanging around his neck because he had seen two little birds hopping around the bar, all right.

Everyone laughed again.

Meanwhile, the flock of sparrows is coming out of the warehouse, prompting him to point his finger in that direction, screaming:

"Look there, you assholes! See? There's four! There's five! Now there are six! No, there are more than ten! Holy shit, there's a flock coming our way! "

Everyone was laughing loudly.

"What the hell is that, Raphael?" Shouted the sailor, standing up, glass in hand, amazed to see dozens of sparrows flying in a circle above all of us, on the tables, and then scattering to the street, while the old man, dumbfounded, was still shouting:

"My-God in Heaven, but what has happened to you, Saint Raphael? Have you become Saint Francis of the Sparrows? "

"They're my friends, too! "

"All right, all right, but did you need to lock them in here to make them drink the water that the little bird won't drink? "

Ralph just laughed with admiring satisfaction, all the while serving the little beat while explaining that the boys had the storm pickups.

"Storm? What storm?" The sailor was surprised, again.

"You didn't see anything? "

"What storm? I think the friend next door is right to question, I who drink and you who get drunk! "

"It was early in the morning. "

"Early morning? Why, I was in town, I was telling you early, but I didn't see any storm! "

"It was quick. "

"You're the delusional ones," he declared, and after emptying the last sip already looking down the street, he added meditatively:

"Every once in a while it would be nice to get some rain. I can't stand this hellish heat!"

And in a sudden flash of memory, he became to them all to continue with the unfortunate matter of that motor on his boat. This time, however, he remembered that he would have to buy a replacement part and make the damn thing work properly, another loss he had incurred. Of course, he didn't let it go unnoticed. He took the opportunity to dishonor Alencar's reputation, calling him a shameless scoundrel for cheating him with the sale of a defective engine. Without forgetting to pick up his glass, he added that he had never seen rain this time of year. Finally, he ended up calling everyone countless liars, scoundrels, just like the idiot Alencar. Yes, not even Ralph escaped. He said he had no shame in his face for converting the birds to the Franciscan habit, while secretly serving alcoholic beverages to these innocent sparrows.

"Well, well, tell me another one, Rafa" he concluded laughing, "just don't bring me birdseed in place of the prickly cheese!"

Rafa's bar was just like that, full of surprises and high spirits of a fun people, all with a keen sense of humor, often of intense energy, passion, and above all, spontaneously funny. On weekends, the bar became a lively attraction. Famous people came from everywhere, yes, bohemians, poets, musicians, writers, players, samba dancers, dubbers, magicians, even crooks, and of course also hunters and fishermen, and many liars. To tell the truth, as a rule, Rafa's bar was considered the best bar in Ilha do Governa-dorMaybe in Rio de Janeiro, might be in the country, this was not an exaggeration to think or believe, without any doubt, it was a bar known by everybody, everywhere.

THE DISASSEMBLER

João Carlos was really a very funny person. Not because he was from São Paulo living in Rio, which was why he had to fly to see his father almost every weekend. There was nothing funny about this, least of all to his father, every time he pulled out his bank statement at the end of the month. Not true, it somehow messed with his head a bit in terms of relationships with his poorer friends, who wouldn't leave the neighborhood, let alone travel to another city. He was funny naturally, that is, without even having to make any stage effort. If one could understand by the way things were compared, it would sound like that actor, who, apparently a playwright, ended up making us laugh without even having any intention of being a little funny himself. Well, if I say all this, it is because decades ago he had started his studies in electronic engineering at the University of Fundão Island. In the first week, however, he got lost on campus and ended up taking mechanical engineering classes believing these were electronic engineering classes…

No, he was not an idiot, far from it, I would even be upset if I knew that my neighborhood friends were making snide remarks about his intelligent personality. In fact, on this student occasion, he was a genius in the flesh, above all a great partner, an extraordinary human figure. Well, a little crazy, yes, true, but a normal crazy. Maybe that's even why he was funny when he was dating Angelica. A beautiful girl from the neighborhood, with whom he spent a lot of time talking like a vulture in love. While all of us, the other neighborhood friends, perfect bums with nothing to do during the day, were distracted by a greasy card game at Ralph's Bar.

However, the unforgettable day — in case the noble reader still thinks I am exaggerating — was the fact that I witnessed it on a Sunday afternoon, a day, by the way, when we usually went to Angelica's house just to chat. So, as the conversation continued, he eventually learned that the television set was not working.

"But I can fix it!" He said, jumping out of the chair, excitedly.

"Really?" Doubted one of us.

"Of course, little guy," he said, already folding his sleeves as he reminded us of his technical skills in electronic engineering high school.

"Well, that being the case, I'll go in the bedroom and get the device," said Angelica's older brother, getting excited with almost childlike animosity.

The TV was then brought and placed on the living room table in front of all of us. João Carlos, now in possession of a Philips screwdriver, immediately unscrewed the lid and all of us, perfect ignorant idiots, just stood around spying on that very complicated electronic system.

"The technology is fantastic, it looks like the aerial view of a space city, doesn't it?" Commented Angelica's younger brother, smiling in admiration at the set of valves and all those transistors.

João Carlos, although he suddenly seemed somewhat worried or insecure about the challenge of fixing the device, upon hearing such a comparison, laughed with an air of debauchery as he poked his finger in everything.

"Don't worry, João, he has the imagination of an astronaut, that's because he lives on the lunar world," commented the older brother, with worse sarcasm.

"I can't even express myself freely," grumbled the younger one back.

"Poor little guy" laughed the older one.

João Carlos continued to ruminate, rattling on; he really looked like a smart ass.

"I hope he can fix this drug, next week the World Cup starts," said the middle brother.

"This time without Pelé", reminded the younger brother.

"Yes, it will be a tough fight," confirmed João Carlos, busy, focused.

"No World Cup will ever be the same as the 1970 World Cup," I said, standing behind everyone.

"Yes, even old Maya painted his bald head greenish yellow!"

"Each Cup differs from one another," observed the middle brother.

"That may be true, but..."

"Where's the electrical outlet?" asked João Carlos, plugger in hand, interrupting me.

"Over there", indicated the older man.

"Let me plug it in," said the middle one, trying to be nice.

"No need, I'll plug it in myself, thanks."

"You're welcome, thank you."

"That's fresh," scoffed the younger one.

"We're all well-educated, thank God," said the middle brother, retorting.

"I don't know, sounds like pure interest to me."

"Be careful, João, don't go into shock," Angelica warned, worried because she feels a natural fear of seeing these electronic things.

"Leave it to me, my love, everything is under control," he reassured, stretching the wire.

"Still, be careful, darling."

"My goodness, what a big deal just because of an electrical outlet," the younger man continued to tease.

"That's affection, my son, affection," Angelica replied, spelling it out syllable by syllable.

"That's right, look at the education, nobody lowers the level here," cautioned the little older man.

Smiling, João Carlos plugged in the plugger, and we all stepped out from behind the device and waited for the picture to appear. Then he pressed the button.

Well, to cut the suspense short, as soon as the image opened, there was a muffled noise, like the shorting of a bare wire, enough to make everyone jump back a step.

"Wow, what a fright, I thought it was going to explode!" Shouted Angelica with her hands on her face, wide-eyed.

"Fuck, now it's fucked for good!" Shouted the middle brother, amazed, looking in my direction.

"It's none of my business, it was his idea!"

"What now? How are we going to watch the Cup?"

"That's nothing, you dear son of a bitch, the worst thing is to go without watching Lost In Space!" Said the younger one, outraged.

We all looked at him suddenly in surprise.

"What's the big deal? It's a good series!"

"Now I see why you imagine space city on electronic devices." Shouted the oldest, laughing.

João Carlos, totally surprised by this unfortunate situation, still tried to explain himself by babbling technical words, a possible overload. Well. It didn't matter, I couldn't even remember what he had said, but whatever the problem was, it was all over. After all, it didn't matter, everyone there now only exchanged insults with each other, such was the anticipation of the previous moment and the frustration generated afterward.

"Fuck it, what the hell!"

"Now what?"

"Now we're fucked!"

"Let's stop this nonsense!"

"Filth is what the fuck, we're out of TV!"

"It was already broken, you piece of shit!"

"Stop swearing, more respect please!" It got attention, Angelica.

Finally, to reassure his brothers (they looked like childishly irritated brutes), Joao Carlos decided to say that he would take the TV to his house. This way he would have more time to find out what the problem was, but he also added that he would bring another TV while he analyzed this one later. Obviously, they all approved of the idea with wide grins from ear to ear, and I even reconsidered the younger brother's sarcasm when he had called them all multiple self-interested people.

I went with João Carlos to get the television. We took a cab with the device in our arms and me sitting in the back. It did not take long to arrive. It was located in Jardim Guanabara, the most extravagant part of the island. In fact, the house was very presentable, architecturally speaking of course, very nicely decorated with wicker chairs and hanging plants on the front porch. We entered from the side of the yard, following a narrow path to the back, where, up ahead, a Cocker dog braided itself around my legs, almost taking me to the ground with braces and all. My luck was Dolores, the housekeeper. She had appeared now, holding her in her lap with hugs and caresses, as in vain had João's curses of accusing the dog of being a carburetor thief, a comment I didn't understand exactly what he meant. Finally, we moved the television to a small room next to the laundry room, on the wall opposite the kitchen door. There is, then, I could, a metal shelf with other televisions; there were also other appliances like mixers, blenders, radios, amplifiers, and many, many other electronic items spread out on a countertop.

"Boy, that's impressive," I muttered in amazement, "that was the very image of electronic chaos!"

I had soon to perform that he had made this place his research laboratory even before he had started his degree in electronic engineering, so I had also concluded that he was a scientist on the verge of madness. But the worst was yet to come. Yes, this was not an exaggeration! Because while João Carlos was picking up the other television — a medium-sized portable device, so no help was needed. I was waiting, looking at an old motorcycle, completely disassembled, by the outer wall of the room, now understanding all his cries accusing the dog of being a thief: there were many parts and screws scattered on the floor so that I immediately assumed that she was taking parts from the bike, leaving João Carlos furious, running after the animal.

When he came back from inside the house with the portable TV in his arms, I decided to ask him if he was also fixing motorcycles.

"That's right, little boy (he always used this expression), that's right, little boy, I've been tinkering with it too."

"Like you did a while ago with the TV?"

"Yes, indeed, I've been trying to understand the mechanism of everything, so I took the motor apart last week."

"I guess the mechanics classes bewitched you, didn't they?"

"Yes, they were good classes, interesting, but the problem is in the reassembly."

"What do you mean? You can't put it back together again?"

"That's right, little guy," he tried to explain as he better straightened the TV in his arms, already walking back down the side hallway of the house, saying:

"I couldn't find some pieces, but I'll still find out where they are, it's just a matter of time, patience, it's because my dog has been stealing smaller pieces, I don't know, she's done it before, you know? I think she's been burying the carburetor just to mess with me, a son of a bitch, that's what she is!"

I trailed after him, with a mad desire to laugh. Something like this was not possible. Unbelievable, the man had gone crazy!

"Were you even able to figure out the malfunction?"

"The Pane? Well, my man worse wasn't that. Worse, that it was working fine," he said, opening the gate and stepping out onto the sidewalk.

I couldn't hold him back. I laughed, surprised.

He didn't even care. He continued, explaining.

"You know, little man, I've been watching some 'classics' of mechanics, and I found it very fascinating!"

I continued to burst out laughing.

"Okay, you may find it funny, but the truth is, little man, I was also excited about mechanics! Can you understand that? Scientific curiosity, that's all, little man, that's all!"

"I think our friends at the bar are absolutely right to call you an idiot," he laughed non-stop.

"Okay, I may be an idiot, but now the situation is really tragic, there's no way out: either I pull myself together and get my stuff back, or else I'm going to end that bitch's run for good!"

We took another cab.

During the ride, I did my best to stop laughing. Indeed. I had managed to do it at first, quieter, but every time I saw a motorcycle pass us. I laughed when I noticed that he stood on his worried face to look behind me as he repeated, not revealing what he had just seen at his house.

"Promise?"

"I'll think about your case," I said, laughing.

"If Angelica's brothers find out, they'll kill me, little guy!"

"Okay, I promise! "

Back at Angelica's house, we went to the living room to install the new device. Sure enough, Angelica's three brothers, two of them already biting their nails, looking scared, were waiting for us with a certain amount of anxiety on their faces. Evidently, this time we all gave a certain distance while he, courageously, promptly stood on the wall to become on the new television. Angelica, just in case, had stayed further back, almost at the hesitate door, ready to run if necessary.

Nyway, I don't want to spoil it, the worst had not happened; yes, amazingly, it had all worked out, and all that air of suspense had disappeared from our expressions, and so we could see the picture without any fear.

"Look," said the younger brother, mesmerized, "has new commercial!"

"Stop talking nonsense, they didn't take an hour!" Shouted the older brother, no longer having the patience to endure his comments.

"Look, the monitor is small," noted the middle one.

"You too, don't say anything!"

"Okay, just a little small".

"Better than nothing, idiot," replied the younger one.

"There's a ghost," said Angelica, taking the risk of saying it, as she walked out the door.

"Nothing serious," said the younger one.

"Must be a valve," commented the middle one.

"Don't make it up, for God's sake!"

"It's an antenna, I'll fix it", said João Carlos.

"No need, my love, we can see everything very well", said Angélica, worried, quickly returning to the door.

"It's just a fit!"

"Careful!"

"When will the other TV be ready?" wanted to know the older young man, also moving away a little.

"Well, dear, the other one..., yeah, dear, first I will need to find out the problem with more patience, you know how things are, dear, that takes some time, some tests. I'll need to disassemble it and..."

I had to rush out of the room, going straight to the bathroom, so I could urgently wrap my face in a felt towel and thus, without guilt, be able to let out a loud, suppressed laugh from my chest. Well, João Carlos was very funny. He was my friend, besides. I had committed myself to the person. It was a promise made, promise fulfilled, the towel was all drooled, I returned to the bedroom after taking a serious look at myself in the mirror, saying, frequently:

"I won't laugh, I give my word."

ON THE ZOMBIE RAMP

Almost every afternoon I would dive off the Zumbi ramp. It was next to the Jequié Iate Club, where I was a 100-meter Crow swimmer. However, swimming at the Zumbi ramp was better. I felt freer because there was not the physical limit of the Olympic pool, strictly that rectangle of monotonous comings and goings. Moreover, the ramp friends were not the same friends as the swim group, except for Nelio, who was on my team; however, the others in the ramp swam just as well as the others in the pool. These friends were part of the groups from the neighborhoods around the island. Night fishing with a trawl net. It was nothing less than the fun gathering of several of us together by the sea. In short, a youth of which most of our parents lived this way, and now, with a certain native pride, also felt the same pride to see us swimming like them. Not exactly as they lived back then because the Guanabara sea in the late 1970s was already different, in a way. At that time, it was very common for oil cargo ships to wash their holds under the pressure of salt water drawn in by injection pumps, releasing excess oil from the holds into the sea. And when this happened, the oil always ended up on the beaches, painting everything in its path with black smoke. It was an ecological disaster (a term that was not even talked about at the time). No one went into the sea, nor did we go near the coastal rocks. A small stain on the skin was enough to have, afterward, a big chemical job to remove it under the shower. That is why, even in those days, it was also very common to taste diesel oil in the mouth while swimming in the bay. It is true that our parents had not had this taste when they were boys swimming at Rampa do Zumbi, a village predominantly inhabited by many Portuguese settlers who fished south of Ilha do Governador. Even so, it was still a good place to swim lightly, without the frequent swells of the open sea. In addition, there was still plenty of trawling and reed fishing, giving a varied number of large fish for our lunch or dinner. The porpoises lived playing in these waters, and in an underwater way, of course, were always warning us that Guanabara Bay still maintained. Even so, it was still a good place to swim lightly, without the frequent swells of the open sea. In addition, there was still plenty of trawling and reed fishing, giving a varied number of broad fish for our snack or dinner. The porpoises lived playing in these waters, and in an underwater way, of course, were always warning us that Guanabara Bay still maintained regular health, and no chemical evil could infect us until then.

So, we learned to see and feel these oceanic facts because we were half land and half sea. It was one of those afternoons, more precisely a Sunday afternoon, when, feeling halfway out to sea, I decided to take my *Corcorocas*[6] fishing rod with me. I think it was about two o'clock in the afternoon when I knocked on the front door, heading for the ramp. I remember it was Sunday because on that day, unlike normal days, many people from northern Rio de Janeiro come to spend the weekend on the island's beaches. So, when I arrived at the shore, even if I didn't know what day it was, I would have known it was a Sunday afternoon by the number of people we didn't usually see during the week. So, I decided to change my mind and put fishing aside. Yes, they would have already scared away every kind of fish that was among submerged rocks. As I approached the crowd, I noticed a family with a pickup truck parked at the curb line next to the

---

[6] Fish about 45 cm long, yellowish body with clear blue streaks,dark dorsal and caudal fins, very common on the Brazilian Coast.

club; behind the car, a fat, smiling woman was preparing sandwiches with soft drinks served in several disposable cups. She, seeing me drive by, smiled maternally. The radio was playing a cheerful samba at high volume, filling the weekend atmosphere. Sundays always ended like this, with this happy, festive image of people from the suburbs enjoying themselves by the seaside.

Then, from the low wall of the pier, on the left side to the ramp by the anchorage, I jumped onto a fishing boat. There were many boats on the long line of the pier. They were secured in bow and stern moorings, preventing them from bending or struggling with each other. These boats belonged to the Portuguese people in the neighborhood. They didn't like anyone climbing on them, except known residents, who, in a communal and supportive way, helped protect them from strange invaders. So, feeling at home, I jumped on top of one of them and settled in beside the helm, already sensing something different on the surface of the water. It was too dark, darker than usual, and that meant, in addition to swimmers bellyaching that burned the skin, that there would be nothing but icy oil sludge rising from the pasty bottom of the sea with the constant roaring and diving.

I was considering to become back when I saw a man kicking a white rubber ball, the kind you can always easily find in supermarkets. He kicked it hard into the sea. The ball went up, and the wind blew in the same direction, causing it to fall further away from the ramp, giving the impression that it was not for this reason, the wind, but the fact that he kicked it spectacularly.

"Did you see that?" Shouted the fellow to the boy next to him.

"Now what?" Asked the boy, worried about the ball.

The fellow smiled, giving the impression that the ball would not be lost. He stepped back with an agile pull and dove quickly into the sea, then pulled in a strong stroke, and there where I stood I could observe his not-so-skillful way of swimming. I also looked at the ball. There was a superficial current caused by the wind that had moved it a little farther away from where it had fallen. Despite this, he swam with some speed due to the strength of his arms, overcoming the incorrect way of swimming. I looked again at the movement on the ramp and saw the boy, now amused among the others. Besides, I was no longer paying attention to the swimmer, when I suddenly felt someone jumping on the boat because of the swing he had made. I looked to the bow. It was Nelio, appearing on the port side, always there for a change.

"Fishing?" he wanted to know, as he pulled the tin bucket over to sit on the edge next to me. He was wearing a white cap.

"Where did you get that?"

"It's my uncle's."

"You look like a shipping tycoon," I joked.

He pretended not to hear, not to care.

"You still haven't caught anything?" He joked, laughing at my Sunday catch.

"I haven't even wet my line yet."

"What a false fisherman!"

"I forgot", he said, justifying the day, looking at the sea, when, suddenly, I didn't see the man who should have been close to the ball.

"Wow, where is he?" I said in sudden astonishment.

"Who?"

The ball was now close to a two-masted sailboat. The current had pulled it forward, where, almost next to the white hull of that sailboat anchored outside the pier, it had lost speed, becoming immobile, almost invisible by the vessel's shadow.

"Didn't he go back to the ramp?"

I looked quickly towards the ramp, but the noise of many people continued in the same way; however, I couldn't find the boy anymore. There were many of them, some very similar to each other. I tried to recognize him and also the man who kicked the ball, although

I was sure I was unable to find him there, after all, the ball was still in the sea.

"I wonder where he got to?"

"He must have dived to the other side of the sail-boat", commented Nélio, already showing little interest in that missing guy.

"Really?" I murmured, thinking about that possibility, too.

"Clear! How many times have we done this? Don't sweat your brains, he must be clutching the bumper tires on the other side of the deck!"

That may be true, but the ball was still close to the hull line, almost at the stern tip. The anchor rope was taut while the other was at the tip of the bow, making me feel any human absence around the sailboat because I didn't hear the noise of people swimming.

"Was it at the party?" asked Nelio, who had already stopped looking for someone he hadn't even seen before.

"I did," I replied without taking my eyes off the ball.

"Was Linen there?"

"Yes."

"He's dating Rita, isn't he?"

"Yes he is."

Nelio became impatient, I soon noticed without taking his eyes off the boat, without paying much attention to what he was saying, despite having a premonition of the reason for his peripheral questions; It was then, swinging my legs over the edge, simultaneously examining the sky, the sailboat, the ball, that he suddenly asked me:

"She was there?"

"Who?"

"Luiza, who else could it be?"

"Not."

"As I already imagined, she spent the weekend in Niterói."

Nobody on the ramp seemed the least bit concerned about the man's disappearance. Everything was as before. Dozens of bathers were diving into the sea all the time. I went back to look at the sailboat. No sign besides the ball, floating near the hull. Was he really that tired?

"This is very strange."

"Strange what?"

"The guy disappeared!"

"Are you still looking for him?"

I did not answer. I kept an eye on the sailboat, I couldn't believe it, he swam well, he was self-confident.

"He must be far away by now," said Nélio, showing little interest.

"And would you leave the ball?"

He looked at me.

"Do you think he drowned?"

"I don't know," I replied hesitantly.

"I don't think so, he must be there."

"He swims well, despite having his head well above water."

"It's the most common defect", said Nélio with disdain; then he changed his tone, as if a sudden idea had just occurred to him.

"How about we go there?"

"Are you willing? The water is cold, very heavy", I inquired seriously.

"Holy shit, I'm not talking about going after that asshole, Dan!"

"Where then?"

"At Luiza's house, man! Who else?"

"Didn't you say she's in Niterói?"

"Yes, I did, but it doesn't hurt to have a look, does it? Maybe she's already back."

"I am not interested."

"Oh, come on, man?" he insisted angrily.

"Already said."

"Aren't you going to tell me you're waiting for the guy to show up from the bottom of the sea? You're still looking for him, aren't you? Stop imagining things, you look stupid."

I didn't say anything, but kept looking at the sailboat, the ball, the ramp...

"Then? Shall we go there or not?"

I was not at all interested in this preposterous idea. Well, what was he up to? I had been bored with this Luiza story for some time now, all that was left was to say her name underwater too. In the 100-meter dash practice, he talked about her the whole time. Was he trying to provoke me? I thought about it while deciding yes or no to accompany him; before I could say anything to that effect, however, he got up quickly, grabbed my pole from the deck, and waited for me to do the same. I didn't move.

"Come on!" He insisted.

Then he followed the narrow deck path, jumping back down to the dock. I was afraid of hurting him at that moment; I hated that insistence because I always thought he could convince me of anything he decided to do. Finally, I was willing to follow him again, so I was more angry with myself than with him. I climbed the wall of the pier, and we started walking along the path along the bank.

We were close to the ramp, where, again, I went back to look for the boy. Holding on, however, Nelio had to wait for me, at which point he complained impatiently, adding that no one was looking for him but me. In fact, everyone there was entertained on the ramp, without any manifestation that raised any apparent suspicion or concern. On the other hand, maybe he had gone out, as Nelio had said without showing any doubt, I thought as he reviewed out the sea to the curve of the beach; there, in that direction, were many coastal rocks dividing the next neighborhood from ours. Yes, why not? We did it that way, swimming to the rocks, where the beach started, it seemed logical but, what about the ball? Why would he leave the ball on the sailboat? Why, who knows, possibly he had lost sight of her while swimming, giving up looking for her because he believed he had gone with the current of the tide! No, it was still very strange, very sinister, strange…

"Let's go, man!" shouted Nelio, further away from me. I quickened my pace toward him, leaving the ball, the man, the sailboat, leaving everything behind.

When I approached Nélio, he went back to talking about Luiza.

"Look, listen, you know what? I think she doesn't like me. It is true! Do not believe?" He asked, noticing my smile.

"It's not like that, Nélio. You look like a bitch in heat" I clarified.

"I didn't know dogs were in heat!"

"You understand," I said, laughing at his face for wanting to play seducer just to make me jealous.

"Look what you're going to say about Luiza, huh!"

"I don't know about her," he said, now really wanting to piss him off.

"Don't know what?"

"I don't know, but as for you, I still believe what you said!"

"How about you, huh? How about you?" He retaliated by adjusting his ridiculous cap.

"What about me, man? Speak up! What about me?"

We were next to the side sidewalk of the club, where the truck was still parked. The sandwich woman was dozing in the back seat. Farther or farther from the sea, he could still hear bathers jumping off the ramp; it was presently, in fact, that I noticed Zé Ferro[7] (he had this nickname due to the braces on his teeth). He was with the others and didn't news that the two of us were passing by Luiza, already a little nervous. I wanted to call him, but Nelio, worried about my inattention and delay, kept reaching for my arm to speak.

"Okay," he said at last, stopping in his tracks for a moment, "okay, I see you took today to screw with me!"

"It's not about that, Nelio," he said, almost shouting. "I'm fed up with this subject! I don't want to know about this anymore, understand?"

"Okay, got it!" He said, adjusting his cap, examining the lead wrapped in the reed he had in his hands, then saying:

"Better this way! Better, I won't need to talk about that other subject."

"What other matter?"

"Like what other matter? Already forgot?"

"If you tell me, I can remember!"

[7] Iron

"It's okay, Dan", he said seriously, "I'm not going to talk about Luiza anymore! Not after what I tell you now! I would like you to listen to it just one more time because I will not repeat myself!"

"Is that the issue? I've already finished! I don't want to talk about her anymore!"

"That wasn't true, man!"

"It does not matter now!"

"You're being more stupid than her, you know that?" He yelled, losing his temper.

"And you, huh!" I screamed too.

"No need to say I'm a bitch in heat!"

"Worse than that! You are nothing but an idiot!"

"I told you, man, I didn't know she was there! There were many people, you see!" He said, distressed, trying to justify himself. He continued.

"Look! How could I have guessed? It is true! I didn't realize she was beside us!"

"Did you need to make that comment?"

He said nothing, looked down, fidgeting with the tip of the pickaxe in his hands. In fact, we were irritated, both hurt by each other.

"Enough of this subject, Nelio", I said, summarize my pace towards the avenue.

"Wait, man!"

"I'm tired, don't you see? Then, you've been wagging your tail after her, haven't you? That was your trick, wasn't it? Well, congratulations, you managed to separate us!"

At the corner, after he had rejoined me, he started talking again while we waited for the cars to pass.

"Listen, Dan," he said, straightening the lead from the coiled line. "Listen… but, first, take this fisherman's rod, I'm already getting bored with this thing", and passed the rod, then continued to say:

"What I want to explain, you still haven't let me talk. No! You don't have to tell me you don't want to hear about it anymore! I know, I talk too much, it's true, but I'm aware of everything I'm saying to you, you heard me? It was not my intention!"

Tried to cross to the other side of the avenue when he grabbed my arm to continue talking.

"Listen, Dan," he said forcefully. "I also recognize when I'm being stupid with my friends! You have been dating her for many years, haven't you? Everyone says, by the way, that you will still end up getting married! It is true! This is nothing new to anyone, least of all me. Do not wait! Let me tell you one more thing. That day at the club, she was just using the same weapon that you used too, did you know that? Yep, that's right, man. Because when she found out about your making out, she was furious, it's obvious. Afterward, when we were at the club (you had already broken off the relationship), she called me aside, in tears, and asked me to stay with her to play a jealousy game with you, do you understand? Do you understand what I'm trying to tell you?"

"I can not believe this!" I screamed as I writhed out of his grasp.

"It's true, man!"

"You were kissing, I saw it!"

"She was mad at you, Dan! She didn't expect him to stay with Carmen! Don't you understand that? So, who? With your best friend! Well, what did you expect, huh? For her to react with empathetic kisses? She already suspected! I wasn't the one who reported! I swear not, man! And when she saw that you were in the club already looking at us, she suddenly pulled my neck and kissed me! Hearing! I know you still like Luiza. That's why I'm telling the truth. We are friends..."

Suddenly, her eyes filled with tears, holding back the emotion of held back tears.

"Yeah, fine, I like her too..." He continued. "You know that, well! But I wasn't even thinking about it, seriously, I didn't even news that minute of the kiss, I even thought I could conquer her, Dan, I admit it..." He would say in a brief effort to find the voice that had disappeared from within him; however, with eyes filled with tears, he added:

"I realized the mistake later, she was just using me to get back at you!"

He took a deep breath. The cars had stopped passing by at that moment, but I couldn't leave the place. I didn't know what to say or what to think, everything was happening so fast, there was no way to reason, such was the state of uncertainties and emotions.

"Don't be stupid with her, man," he continued speaking, his voice lighter now. "Can't you see she adores you? And if I'm telling you all this it's because, despite the love I feel for her, I want you two to be happy! It wouldn't work for me at all! When we were together, she only talked about you, all the time! Yes, that's right, I've always wanted to know what you think, what you say, even what you like to do most when you're not with her, all that was missing was asking if you masturbated thinking about her! Dust! Which is? I'm not a masochist! It makes me suffer, you understand! How could I feed the feeling I have for her when, in fact, she feels for you? No, I would only suffer more and more, and destroy our friendship too! As you can see, my dear, love has to transcend all that! She loves You! My love, by itself, therefore, could not become a hindrance to anyone, least of all to me! That's why I told you that I'm aware of everything I tell you now, I would be acting hypocritically, being dumber than you are being reciprocally! She loves you, not me! That's the truth!"

I froze, looking at him like a wretched idiot, a wretch of feelings.

"Well, that was the other subject I wanted to talk to you about," he continued. "I think I managed to say it all. I won't talk about it anymore, but I sincerely hope you make the right decision. After all, happiness in love is a rare feeling when two people meet on this planet of sentimental egoists; you need to think about it for sure."

I was speechless, stunned. His words, for the first time (although I didn't understand all of this at first), produced a twist in my head, in my thoughts. I was already crossing the avenue, when he quickly added:

"Tomorrow you will look for her and justify yourself, you heard me right!" You won't need to forgive her for anything, but if there is a need, the first person to forgive is yourself! Do not forget."

"Okay," I replied stunned, swallowing hard.

I was already close to home while I was thinking about how I should talk to Luiza from now on, when, suddenly, Zé Ferro, coming from the beach, still wet from the sea, called me running to receive me. I stayed at the gate of the house, waiting for him.

"Did you see the crowd that gathered on the ramp?" He immediately wanted to know as he approached.

"Today is Sunday," I clarified.

"That's not what I'm talking about, someone drowned! They noticed because they saw a ball next to the sailboat King (who was the sailboat's name)!"

After catching his breath and spitting the diesel taste off his tongue, he continued:

"Then they saw the ball right at the helm, can you believe it? Man, it was hell! The drowned man's mother was sleeping in a van when they rushed to report that he was missing. I think it was the nephew who said he swam to the sailboat and then couldn't find it anywhere. Damn it, had to see the woman, she nearly lost her mind! She wanted to go into the sea and help her son! Many people had to run after her! She really wanted to jump into the sea as soon as possible, imagine! Well, no one has found it yet! There's no way of knowing if he sank at that moment, or before, so the current must have already carried the body, far away... he seems to suffer from epilepsy..."

He paused, saw that I was there because of the fishing rod in my hands. After another spit, he said:

"Well, as this sea is not for fish, I decided to let the Portuguese man at the bar know. They said the marine rescue team would arrive shortly thereafter. I don't know, apparently it will be the IML[8] hearse that will arrive first"

He spat the diesel off his tongue and continued:

"I thought you saw it... Well, it doesn't matter, you didn't know how to do anything either, even though you're one of the best swimmers in Zumbi," he said,

[8] Legal Medical Institute

wanting to reassure me; then, making an expression of regret, he added sadly:

"Now he's really dead, poor mother."

My eyes were blurred with tears, I felt my throat hurt. When I found myself, Zé Ferro had disappeared. I hadn't even noticed. I wasn't even sure who I was holding back my tears for. My sadness hurt, my feelings were in shambles, I didn't know what else to do or think. In fact, I didn't know anything about myself anymore.

A RESTLESS NIGHT

I

When the night approached me, bringing with the breeze the scent of date palms coming from the endless wilderness, it also brought my friend to my door.

"Can you accompany me to Ribeira?" He wanted to know, with his face stuck between the openings.

"For what?" I asked, opening the door.

"I want to go to Julia's house, get a book I borrowed" he replied without entering.

"Júlia..." he said thinking, trying to remember that name.

"You don't know her, she's my student classmate."

I went out to the porch.

"But why do I have to go with you?"

He put his arm around my shoulders to whisper

"I'm dating her, nothing serious, you understand? But you need to help me, Dan", he said, smiling a bit awkwardly.

"Help in what?" I asked, surprised.

He took his arm off me; in so doing he greatly relieved my nostrils: his shirt gave off a cloying perfume.

Then he descended the step and went to the gate.

"Well, Dan, only you can do that for me," he said again, pulling himself up with his arms and sitting on the railing. I went down from the porch and went to sit next to him, already intrigued by the sinister conversation.

"I still do not understand."

"She's engaged to a guy who's a bit of a bully", he continued, although at that moment he interrupted what he was starting to explain already wanting to remind me who he was, saying he was a guy with Apache Indian hair who was always on the beach in Zumbi, playing volleyball.

"No, I don't know who it is," I said, thinking.

"Well, it doesn't matter," he resumed the subject, "the fact is that he's very jealous, even though he's already suspicious of me." But luckily for us, he doesn't know me, but he knows I exist and that I hit on her, you know?

"Wait a minute, our luck?"

"Actually, what he really wants is to hit me just because he's being beaten by my brother!"

"What I have to do with it?"

"Just telling you, that was it!"

"Just because of that?" I asked wryly, still amazed.

"That was before. The two fell out at the bar! The man is always filling the tubes, then he gets in trouble! My brother, you know, he's bad-tempered, he beat him up, and now he wants to get back at me!"

"This is bad, you're going to get your ass kicked," he said, still stunned by the revelation.

"Fuck? Me?"

"Yes, you! And you'll get hit a lot, I wouldn't even want to be in your shoes! See? Besides knowing that you're the brother of the man who took the hit, now he's also hitting on your wife! Wow, Luiz, Jesus Christ, man, anyone would be mad!"

"Oh, come on, Dan? Now you want to defend the enemy?"

"What an enemy if I don't even know who you're talking about!"

"I just said, fuck you! He's nothing but a bastard, an asshole, a coward! Moreover, Julia says he's pull the boundaries!"

"Then why doesn't she just end the engagement at once?"

"That's it! Don't you pay attention? He's pull the envelope! She's scared to break up with him, obviously! Blackmail, threats, can you believe it?"

"Truth?"

"Seriously, I'm telling you, the guy gets beaten up on the street and then takes his anger out on her!"

"So this idiot is crazy!" I said worried.

"Yes, crazy!"

"And you too!"

"Me, why?" He looked quickly at me.

"You're taking too many risks, that's all," I clarified immediately.

He didn't say anything, just looked at me with an expression of astonishment, then become towards the street. He looked down at the asphalt, face in his hands, elbows buried in his knees, seeming to stare only at nothing or the approaching danger.

"Are you liking her?" I asked after watching him silently for a moment.

"I don't know," I said, looking like I didn't want to talk about it.

"Apparently it is."

"It's hard to explain, Dan, but lately, I can't get her out of my head. It's all the time, man!"

"I think you should forget about her, I don't know, things could end badly, Luiz, I said, wanting to warn him."

"It won't end badly, and I'm not here to hear it, Dan! I just want to know whether you can come with me or not, that's all."

Before I could say, "Don't trouble me," a bespectacled passerby approached and asked where the path to the endless jungle was. Luiz, explaining, got down from the wall and indicated the direction he should take. The subject thanked him and followed the indicated path.

"You still haven't said why I should go with you," I said, getting back to the point.

Luiz pulled away and looked at me with a mischievous smile, then said that everything would be simple, adding:

"If the two of us arrive at Júlia's house saying that I just came to pick up a book, he won't suspect anything, if he shows up there, of course!"

"But this book…", I said, reasoning, "couldn't she return this book in the course?"

"Yes, I could," he replied, smiling enthusiastically, "but she is no longer answer I serve classes, reinforcing my argument about the unexpected visit, claiming that I need him!"

"I can't believe it," I said in surprise, "did you think of all this as if by magic?"

"So! Don't you think it's a great, genius idea?"

"Genius? This is crazy, man", I replied, laughing at his naivety.

"Madness, why?"

"So you really think he's going to fall for that nonsense?"

"Well, why not?"

"Because he's already suspicious, honey. Didn't you say that yourself?"

"He doesn't even know me, he doesn't even know who I am", he replied, seriously.

"Do you need it? See, Luiz? If that's the case, everyone is a suspect, including you!"

He pointed his finger at me, flashing the same smile, saying:

"Well, that's where you come into play!"

"I?"

"Oh Dan, nobody goes to a girl's house with another classmate, I mean not when they have ulterior motives of course!"

"I still do not understand."

"You do not see? We are colleagues, we are innocent, we are just passing through, the book, that's what matters ", he said, convinced of his words.

"I can't believe what I'm hearing! You've definitely gone crazy!"

"But..."

"No, but, this is crazy, man. Pure idiocy, you know?"

He didn't say anything, for a few seconds he looked at me with an expression of astonishment, as if he hadn't expected such a negative reaction.

We stayed quiet, just watching the movement of the street, newly illuminated by the mercury lamppost. Passers-by were passing by at that time. They returned from work tired, with sweat drying on their skin, very hot. They came crazy for a bath and something to satisfy their hunger.

"So, how to do it?"

"How to do what?"

"Are you coming with me or not?" He wanted to know as he walked back to the wall, sitting down next to me.

"Not."

"I'll set the time, Dan!"

"Call now!"

"She doesn't have a phone."

"Lie."

"It's true, she doesn't have a phone."

I thought for a moment. The way he was out of control, insistent, this Julia person must have been quite a girl. I hesitated between yes and no. Shit, it all felt so right and wrong at the same time! Apparently, she was already involved with their secret meetings. Yes, I was questioning my role as an idiot. I decided to tell him that if I went with him. I would stand outside like a mischievous sentry Cupid, just watching the executioner approach while they, the two lovebirds, would simply be kissing and cuddling inside the house, maybe even laughing at my idiotic face.

"No way," he replied in serious alarm. "I'm saying I'm going to schedule the next meeting."

"Looks like it," I said, laughing sarcastically.

"I'm serious, this won't take even two minutes."

"I don't believe."

"Ah, what is it, my comrade, you are taking me for a fool, I do not intend to enter her house, I am not such a fool as to make such a mistake, man!"

"Are you serious?"

"Serious!"

"Aren't you going to make a fool of me too?"

"To make a fool of a friend who would accompany me on such a feat..." he said, now seeming to sense my condescension, then added:

"No, not at all, friend, because I might pluck my blackberries and throw them overboard for sharks if I'm lying!"

"All the more reason not to trust you, you bastard," I said sarcastically again.

He continued to stare at me, waiting for the expected answer. In that expectation, I realized that I could no longer retreat.

"Okay, I'll go with you."

"Ah, my friend, I knew you would help me," he said, with a wide smile.

"You will owe me that one!"

"No problem! You never left me, my dear adventure partner!"

"But I warn you: I'm only going to stay two minutes, no more."

"Okay, I swear, you'll see, I'm just going to mark it," he would say, rubbing his hands; and, as he spoke thus, he opened his arms, trying to embrace me, as I sprang from the wall onto the sidewalk.

"That perfume stinks," I said, pinching my nostrils.

"It's strong, isn't it?" He wanted to know, suddenly worried, turning to sniff his armpit, saying he couldn't smell anything.

I was already going through the gate, going up on the porch, letting them know that I would be back soon, I would just get a better shirt.

"Don't delay."

II

We were going to Zumbi beach. The sea was dark and there were no fishermen on the beach. We entered through the stone street. From there, the path continued to the Ribeira area, always with a night view of the sea on the west side as we walked at the same pace. Occasionally, I looked over the lights to the other side of the bay, where, incidentally, I pursued my beach daydreams or dreams of one day being successful in life. Despite having no prospects, only the presentiment of a distant future. Well, an uncertain future ahead, anyway. Even so, there seemed to be hope, one day it might happen. I needed to believe because my existence was lost in the midst of so many thoughts, it was as if I was diving into myself, looking for the best path to follow. Yes, one day, who knows, one day it would emerge from the depths of my life, like the soul of a turtle emerging from the depths of the ocean. Maybe I would bring the answer that would give me the feeling of existing, not giving up on myself...

"What are you thinking?" Luiz asked, walking at the same pace as my steps.

"I? Oh, I don't really know, maybe in life, I don't know," I replied thinking about this also curious question.

"In life? Well, I tell you, Dan, life is full of charms, many surprises...", and, stopping smiling for a moment, he suddenly added:

"Of course, sometimes with unpleasant surprises, but nothing that you can't solve with your head held high, you know? Yes, also in the right place and at the right time, isn't it?"

"Yes", I agreed, thinking about what I had just heard. Though I thought he was a little stupid for saying so. By the way, which made me feel even more stupid, after all I was complicit in the crazy idea of following him to the neighboring neighborhood because of a woman I didn't even know.

"The bad moments have to be overcome, and otherwise we won't be able to enjoy the charms that life gives us over the years, it's true." He said. Now, I thought, immediately I wanted to be an adviser without measure, that it was even more ridiculous to have to listen to him.

A car came from the end of the street. Came from low beam. He walked past us slowly, but soon silence returned. And on this part of the route there were many trees on either side of the sidewalks. The wind, which came from the sea, blew over the leaves, shaking the branches in disarray, releasing the sound similar to light rain through the air.

"You know, Dan," said Luiz, after a brief silence, "one day I'll own a bar; but, you see, this bar will be very different from the bars we are used to seeing around..."

And looking at me intently, he commented that I could be his partner too.

"I don't know, I've been wanting to see the world", I said, not believing what he was saying.

"Which is? You will get tired of traveling, everyone gets tired, even sailors get tired one day too!"

"You might get tired of the bar," I replied.

"I doubt it. Not from this bar! It's a project I've been thinking about for a long time, I'm just telling you now because I'm sure I'll do it!"

"Wasn't there before?"

"No, I mean I did," he said, trying to explain himself further. "I was sure of that when I found out that my brother was going to pass me his. He'll open another one, you know? Yes, it will be in Tijuca!"

"And what will be different?"

"Ah, my friend, you haven't seen that yet", he said more cheerfully, revealing a wide dreamy smile. Suddenly, he added:

"But I can tell you that it will be a bar without tables or chairs!"

"What?" I was startled.

"Wait, that's not what I meant," he said, trying to explain himself further.

"What a crazy idea!"

"The thing is not quite like that, there will be tables and chairs, but made of cement blocks glued to the floor."

I was about to laugh when he added:

"Calm down, I'll explain", he warned, as soon as he noticed my ironic smile, at which point he tried to tell me that while enumerating with his fingers:

"Do you know how many bottles have been broken with all those people around the tables? Over 50 within two years! Do you know how many dishes? Over 40 within six months! This, obviously, without considering the loss of repairing tables and chairs, which had to be replaced in approximately two years."

After the destruction of the bar was over, I continued picking up the broken glass and crockery scattered across the floor of my imagination without even calculating the result of that mathematical explanation. My brain was jumbled with numbers, not understanding how these incidents could happen in a bar so often.

"And the glasses?"

"And them?"

"They also break!"

"For that very reason, everything will be disposable!"

"I think it's horrible to drink beer from a plastic cup."

"Yes, I think so too, but my brother's clientele are real herds walking into a crystal shop!"

I chuckled, finding this comparison amusing.

"But it is true," he continued, "I have never seen such ill-mannered people! That, of course, not to mention the confusion that comes around! Last time, by the way…"

And raising his hand indicating the place that already seemed close, he continued saying:

"Last I heard, what did he do? Haven't I told you yet? Well, then you will fall when I say so!"

He stopped talking for a moment. We had reached the end of the shore, where there was a stone slope that bordered the hill to the Ribeira neighborhood. We then entered another street, steep and narrow, which ended in the main square; as soon as we started a new route that required talking less due to shortness of breath, incredibly he would take up the subject talking more and more.

"Well, that was the day, I was telling you, my brother told him to run! The bar, damn it, the bar was packed with people; but for once, he was there bugging me, believe me he was with Julia; indeed a rare thing to see there; well, isn't it that suddenly, just like that, the soft ass gets up from the table and goes to meet our master of ceremonies, punching him in the face?"

I was surprised to hear that. I met the sambista, a refined guy, very polite. Luiz noticed my astonishment.

"It is true!" He stated. "It was just for the smile he showed her, believe me? My brother, who already disliked him, didn't think twice: he jumped over the counter and started hitting him!"

"And Paulinho?" I wanted to know, referring to the master of ceremonies.

"Him? Well, he lost his swing, of course! Anyway, he and the other sambistas were all defended right there, after all, they are our poets, our composers, people we have a duty to take good care of! "

"You can be sure of that," I agreed.

"This guy is very vain", said Luiz, indignant.

"I didn't know Paulinho had gone through that, poor thing."

"Yes, but let the 'where he at' crowd know about it! That bully will end up in the ditch with his mouth full of ants!"

He stopped talking, took a breath and waited for me to arrive. As we walked up the dark, narrow street, the lights in the square grew bigger and bigger, expanding brighter brightness ahead of us, beyond. I stopped for a moment, looking back toward the sea. There, on full moon nights, we could always enjoy a beautiful view of the bay! But now there was nothing but a dark and starless sky, finally, a moonless night, leading me to believe that it was possibly a restless night that was yet to happen.

"We're close", warned Luiz, a little ahead.

"Does she live around here?" I asked breathlessly.

"No, it's on the other side of the square", he replied, waiting for me to arrive.

I looked back again. We were on the highest slope of the hill. There was no landscape, only distant lights, which, shining on the edge of the small islets, on the other side of the bay, made dotted reflections in luminous lines on the dark mantle of the sea. Besides, the night seemed sad, empty, as if I could sense something bad in the air, perhaps a restless, moonless night...

"Let's go!" shouted Luiz, who was already in the phosphorescent light of the square.

I quickened my pace towards him, still panting. On the other side of the square, we entered through a dark shortcut, coming out on another street with half a dozen houses separated from each other. They were close to the green hillside. As we passed in front of them, the dogs barked, denouncing our presence. Luiz didn't seem worried, he continued at a fast pace, in a good mood. I hurried to accompany him. In fact, I was scared. All those dogs barking in a frenzy, giving the impression of many eyes peering at us through the cracks in the shutters.

"I think we should go back," I said suddenly, chickening out.

"What? After all that walking?"

"He could be hanging around the place, Luiz!"

"No, not here," he said, looking around.

"Who guarantees us?"

"I guarantee."

"I do not know..."

"Anyway, if he's at Julia's, he doesn't forget the deal. Now let's be quiet, we're coming."

Luiz, more exposed, approached the gate of a whitewashed house, on whose outer wall at the entrance to the porch, I saw elongated lines of drained moss, caused by the rains. We didn't go into the courtyard, we stayed parked in front of the gate, for a moment scrutinizing voices that seemed to come from far away, increasing my uneasiness. Then, Luiz, courageously, decided to applaud fervently. There, now, yes, presently all the dogs had really gone mad beyond belief, and the whole neighborhood seemed to be barking too! Suddenly, my saliva dried up, my heart raced. Soon there appeared at the open window, through the gap in the light transparent bluish curtains, a beautiful girl with brown hair! I saw two green eyes shine in her beautiful face. She, however, when she saw us and recognized Luiz, with a start, put her hands to her mouth, whispering in a gesture with mute lips, this question: "Are you crazy"?

"I came to get the book I lent you," he said with the greatest lack of modesty, disguising it, implying that he was a student. Well, frankly, the bandit didn't like to read either a magazine or a dirty comic book just out of laziness!

Well, the romantic couple continued to cover up, chatting from a distance.

"What?" She wanted to know, without yet understanding.

"I have a test next week!"

She then walked back into the room, disappearing behind the curtain that had been released, swaying at night breeze.

Luiz glanced quickly at me, blinking as if to say slyly that he wasn't there. So, she opened the door and went out onto the porch with that book in her hands. When I saw her full length, the pores on her arms and the back of her neck prickled with frank emotion, while I must have muttered something like words of admiration with my heartbeat hammering in my chest; at the same moment, I heard Luiz reply between his teeth: "I also think the same thing". She was very fast, I didn't even have time to run my eyes over her beautiful and passionate body. Luiz went to the balcony, and she handed him the book while repeating the same words she had said at the window, calling him crazy, however, adding that the groom was coming any moment.

"He doesn't know me," assured the idiot.

"But not here," she insisted.

"Where then?"

I didn't take my eyes off her. I continued there on the sidewalk, leaning against the wall, begging in my mind for a second of her gaze. Lasted for a moment, when she peeked at me over Luiz's shoulder, making me imagine I was in his place. Yes, my God, I was possessed, excited, she was a beautiful girl to make anyone crazy with passion. Then, unexpectedly, someone placed a heavy hand on my shoulder, saying:

"I want to talk to you."

He was a tall guy, taller than me. He was shirtless, showing athletic, manly musculature, more athletic and manly than my feigned muscular strength. Not really understanding what was going on there, I suddenly felt surprised.

"With me?"

"That's right," said the guy, who was already out of sight of the house, waiting for me by a tin wall of the building.

I pull away from the wall and went to him. Although I found it all very strange, after all, whoever it was or had something to say to me, it didn't seem to be in a very friendly tone. I had noticed the severe way he was looking at me. When I got close to him, my mind dropped: it was the APACHE I had forgotten.

"Go ahead," I said, hiding my surprised look.

"So you are the Luiz guy?"

"What?" I asked even more surprised, not believing what I had just heard.

"It's you, you imbecile!"

"Me? Not really, man! You're wrong," I said, growing more and more surprised.

"Moron!"

"My name is Dan."

"Dan is badass! Lie down somewhere else!" He shouted, giving me a furious shove on the shoulder:

"You think I'm silly, do you, you asshole?"

"I'm not lying," I said, startled, "my name is Dan Paz[9]..."

"Peace my ass!"

"But it's true!"

"What are you doing here? It's not bad enough your brother has bothered me, now you want to change your name just so you don't get beat up? Because I'm going to teach you not to hit on other people's women, you heard right, you piece of shit from Don Juan!"

He bullied me without listening to what I had to say. Although I was scared, I took my wallet out of my pocket and showed him who I was, saying under his furious jealousy that I wasn't who he thought I was. I could prove it through the ID.

"See, read my name here!" I said with my wallet in my hands.

---

[9] Paz (peace) is also used as a surname.

He would rather not check. He was blind with rage as he hit my hands hard. My wallet flew, scattering my documents across the floor; then, without even giving myself time to think about what to do, I received a very hard punch to the left ear and another to the chin, hitting my back against the zinc wall. The metallic boom drove the neighborhood dogs even more crazy. I tasted oily rust on my tongue. Blood trickled from my mouth between my teeth. I heard a dull buzzing in my head. Everything, simultaneously. In seconds, I received another blow, this time in the stomach, feeling then that I was falling without mass and without weight, passing out before even hitting the ground.

For a few seconds, or minutes, I don't know, I didn't know anything about myself anymore. I couldn't even tell where my conscience was. I had completely disappeared from myself, I had forgotten my name, my identity. Slowly, I came back from the dive with no air in my lungs. I tried to rise to the surface, to emerge. I couldn't feel my limbs. Strangely, I heard voices and barking in the distance. That shouldn't be possible. I struggled not to drown as a figure loomed over my face. Then I understood that I was drowning in my blood. I was lying on my back on the pavement with my legs suspended by this figure. He would fold and unfold my legs, going with his knees on my chest, in a continuous movement of the legs back and forth, without stopping. Slowly, the figure took shape and became Luiz's face, his eyes blurred by tears, he shouted my name without being able to see me and confirm that I had come to myself; when I back the movement of my legs though, he realized that I had been resurrected, so he quickly released them with emotional screams:

"Fucking hell, man, you're alive, thank you, my God, you're alive, my brother!"

I lifted my back off the floor helped by him, but remaining seated by the buzzing head, still everything was spinning dazedly around me. I had to lean against the wall, regain my normal state. Meanwhile, the dogs barked furiously. I looked at the documents spread out on the cobblestones, almost at the curb. Back to reason, I remembered almost instantly what had happened.

"Where did the bastard go?" I wanted to know, putting my hand on my sore chin, feeling the taste of crushed blood in my mouth, my jaw swollen as if I had received a brick in the face, my head buzzing the whole time.

"The animal entered Júlia's house", said Luiz, startled, visibly worried.

I heard more screaming.

"What is happening?"

"The thing got difficult, my friend, the man is breaking everything, inside! The neighbor called the police!"

"Then gather my documents, let's get out of here", I said, getting up from the floor with the support of the wall.

Luiz gathered my documents with the same speed with which street vendors flee from inspectors, but he stuffed them back in his wallet anyway. Dogs were barking all the time, you could hear people screaming in voices mixed with furniture breaking.

"What the fuck is going on?" I wanted to know, looking at the house, unable to see anything.

"The neighbor went there, man," he informed me, handing me his wallet.

"Are they fighting?"

"He lives across the street, the green house," he said, turning and pointing. "He's from the civil police, this time they're going to put him in jail!"

In fact, right after saying that, we saw a police car pulling into our street. It came slowly and with the siren turned off, maybe they didn't want to call the attention of the "peaceful" residents of the neighborhood.

"Let's get up, my friend," he said, stepping forward, crossing to the other side of the sidewalk. I followed behind, running to catch up, when, just in case, we pretended to slow down at the end of the street, also so as not to attract too much attention. The car passed us with its red headlights.

"He's going to get a hard cane", said Luiz, smiling with satisfaction.

III

Leaving this second street, we return to the illuminated square, along the same path going up the slope to the sea, where the sea air eased my pain.

"How did you not understand either?"

"I don't know, Dan," he said, quickening his pace, "the man was really fast! When I came out of the gate, you were already on the ground! The crazy guy walked past me and didn't even realize I was there! He was blind with rage!"

"You're a liar!"

"Liar? I?"

"Did you hide in the closet?"

"What closet, man, what are you talking about?"

"You used me, you piece of shit!"

"I'm telling you, I was on the porch, man," he continued apologetically.

"Didn't you hear the noise?"

"When I went to the gate, he broke up with you! There was no time, that's all!"

"Just that!" I yelled, indignant. "So you couldn't tell him who I was? Who were you? He breaks me, and you tell me about it?"

I had to rest my hand on my chin for the strongest pain. He stared at me with an astonished expression, not saying anything else, just looking at me, scared. My ear throbbed. I slowed down, sat down on the wall that separated the beach from the sidewalk. A bat flew in front of the streetlamp, almost crossing its black wings of death over our heads, then disappeared into the dark, starless, moonless night. Luiz also sat next to me, putting his feet in the sand. He watched the darkness of the sea, where the reflections of colored lights of various shades of neon danced there.

"Are you very upset with me?" He asked after sighing despondently.

"Never mind," I replied sullenly, my swollen jaw hurting, which was worse.

"He's probably already in the van on the way to jail," he said, trying to reassure me.

"It better be, this will be the end of this shitty engagement."

"Well, thereafter, I'm sure you did," he said, looking up from the sea.

"Yes, he got into a fight with the police people, that's worse."

We were silent. The current of dark sea air had changed. I had noticed by the lights reflected in the sea. They grew faster, rippling in bright, misshapen, quivering lines in a continual frenzied frenzy. On the other side of the bay, on the west side, was the small island of water, formerly the island of sword mangoes, whose fruit no longer existed because it now served as an oil base. Several ships were anchored around. They refilled the oil tanks and headed out to sea. I looked up at the sky. Suddenly, the moon appeared from behind the heavy clouds, that was a good sign. I looked at Luis. He remained silent, thoughtful, his eyes lost in the reverie of colored lights, perhaps lost, like me, although he was still curious.

"How did he suspect you were the brother he had beaten up?" I decided to question.

"He found a note in Julia's purse."

"What a mistake to send a passionate note, you idiot."

"It was just a message," he said.

"What message?"

"Just two words: what time, nothing more."

"Then how did he know?"

"The newspaper had the logo of the bar."

"I falter worse!"

"So is."

"You suspected your brother, of course."

"In the beginning, yes, that's why he started showing up at the bar; he must have compared the numerical handwriting and ended up identifying my handwriting from the notes I took in the morning. He saw that it wasn't the same handwriting as my brother's. Only he never saw me, but he knew I existed, right there."

"Did he also know that you studied in the same course as Julia?"

"I thought about it, but Julia assured me he didn't know that."

"She lives alone?"

"No, she lives with her aunt, but she is never there. The family is from Araruama."

"She is very pretty," I ventured to say.

"Yes, she is beautiful, I know."

"Yes, she is beautiful."

"Linda is a nickname!"

"Yes, impressive."

"It is also little."

"Okay, enough with the freshness."

"I also agree, you told the truth there at the gate."

"Yes, tasty."

"It's mine."

"I said nothing."

"I thought, I know."

We were silent again. Suddenly, the wind blew stronger, coming from the top of Morro do Ouro that crossed the hidden orchard, beyond the endless open field, from where the afternoons brought the sweet aroma of ripe date palms to my window.

"Now you won't need to meet her in secret anymore", I said, bending my leg over my knee, already thinking that this would have to be the romance.

"Everything points to it," he agreed, lowering his face, still shuffling his feet in the sand.

My ear was still throbbing. The sore, swollen mouth made me think of an ice pack.

"It's getting late," I said, looking at the dark sky over the lights across the sea. I refrained from giving a yawn due to the pain.

"Yes, it's late."

"We better go home, tomorrow I have an interview with an airline."

We got up ready to go home, still having to walk the long tree-lined sidewalk. We continue in silence...

It was weird. Very strange. I couldn't get Julia out of my head anymore. I looked at Luiz sideways. Surely, he thought of her too. Yes, I knew that, I was sure of it, damn it. I kept thinking about her anyway. That was very strange, I kept remembering her face, her brown hair, her greenish eyes, her lips, her body... Well, maybe I wouldn't think about her when I got home, I thought. Besides, tomorrow would definitely be a better day. Maybe I wouldn't even think about that staring expression anymore, or think about anything else, forgetting about it once and for all. Yes, maybe, just maybe; but, I don't know, tomorrow hadn't come yet; however, what was wrong with that, I might think about her some more, which is the problem because, for now, I couldn't get her out of my head, to the point of not even caring about Luiz's feelings. Well, dammit, it was his fault, he was responsible, he might even interfere with my interview tomorrow… Suddenly, I remembered to check the documents, reaching into my pocket and taking out my wallet. I went through them one by one quickly. Amazing! That couldn't be true, that was a bad sign, I don't know, I just realized with surprise that I would have to go back to Julia's house, I didn't have the identity document! Well, screw that too, I thought. But the lack of the document was worse. Now the memory of Julia's gaze seemed stronger, more intense. I replaced the wallet in my pocket; so I reconsidered going tomorrow night. Perhaps the weather was calmer by then. Possibly, the document was lying beside the curb near the fences. Maybe I could borrow a flashlight from her. What about Luiz? Shit, to hell with Luiz, he chickened out not to reveal his name. My God, I need to stop thinking about her, I wish she didn't have a flashlight, that would be a good start…

"Some problem?"

"What? Problem? No, no problem."

"Is there any document missing?"

"Everything is fine."

"It was all mixed up, confused."

"All right."

"Looks worried."

"Print only!"

"What time are you going there?"

"There? Where?" I asked, suddenly afraid.

"In the interview!"

"What interview?"

"In the interview, man! You forgot?"

"Ah! Yes, the interview, it is!"

"Is it morning?"

"Yes, morning."

"Maybe it will be better by then."

"I suppose so."

"If you don't get the job, I will feel guilty about it."

"Guilty of what?"

"The swelling."

"I feel no more pain."

"Put ice on it when you get home."

"Yes, ice is good."

"You are weird."

"Weird? I? Well, it must be the pain..."

"Are you feeling good?"

"I'm fine, why?"

As we walked along the beach, he kept looking at me out of the corner of his eye the whole time. He looked more suspicious now, very suspicious indeed, giving the impression of trying to read my thoughts. I even had to exaggerate a pain that no longer existed, despite feeling my chin a little sore, my left ear too, but I already felt much more willing.

"Tomorrow I'll be at the bar, on duty."

"Serious?"

"Come by, we'll have a beer."

"I don't know, Luiz, I think I'll take an anti-biotic, so it doesn't get inflamed later."

"Yes, it is still very swollen."

We kept walking, not saying anything mutually. In fact, talking wasn't practical, that could delay the bruise. Not bad, not having to talk, giving many explanations, that was great, I thought…

We were already closer to our homes. I kept thinking. Um, so he'll be on call tomorrow. That was good, too. Night shifts are always necessary, really. Not that I wanted to be opportunistic in thinking that way, no, not at all, not least because being without a document would not be good at all. It would take a long time to provide the second route, the queue moves, time flies, it would end up without work…

We continued walking in silence. The streets were already empty, and our silence was greater than the silence of the neighborhood, it was an oceanic silence. Well, yes, I knew that, during all that time, in silence, he certainly kept thinking about Luiza. Yes, he certainly thought about her all the time, all the time. Well, although I didn't try to watch him so as not to be too conspicuous, I could feel it. Well, get this, I used to think about her too; not the way he thought, of course, I thought more romantically than he did. In fact, I was really hoping she didn't have a flashlight, I had seen the sky, I had seen the white, round moon, rising far away through the gaps in the sparse clouds. That was a good sign, it seemed like a promising warning, the moon always helped my senses, maybe I would be much better by dusk the next day because that would be much better. Possibly, she really didn't have a flashlight, so she decided to help me look for my document under the moonlight…

SECOND PART

BEFORE AND AFTER THE BUS GOES BY

On the horizon, the sun was a little below the sea line when, silently, we started to climb the five floors of the building. I went ahead because the key to the padlock was with me; Dionísio, a childhood friend, climbed behind, followed by his strange friend. Iunlocked the padlock and carefully pull open the door. It was jammed, so it was customary to lift it up a bit, so as not to make that annoying door-sliding noise. We enter the terrace. The morning breeze was blowing, and the horizon bled the white tiles of the top floor of the open terrace orange-red. On the horizon, the sun now rose majestically.

I secretly meditated on the dawn of the sea. He was absorbed in the new light of day, listening to the morning song of the sparrows. Beside me, I cast a brief glance at the two of them crouched against the side wall of the stairs. The two prepared the heroin dose. They brought it in the leather bag. In addition to the powder, a bottle of still mineral water and a used disposable syringe. In silence, they busied themselves with chemically mixing the powder. Whether it was their intention to seek relief or even psychedelic dreams, I don't entirely know. At least I had the social sensitivity to understand that our youth were running from a hypocritical reality worse than this one that caused risky changes in us. From psychological experience, tragic or not, it seemed that the world was also changing. It was the dream of youth in search of broad intellectual emancipation against what had been established for centuries, always the same repetition of the system, although with new guises. Some friends got into this dust stream, and then a lot changed inside all of them. It was as if there were hundreds of other selves hidden inside each of us, I couldn't explain. Maybe I couldn't understand why my world showed more than that. I just didn't know what it was, although I knew that everything was an inexplicable greatness under all phases of life, the clarity of understanding under that prism was enough.

Looked back at the sea. The sun's marine glow was sparkling. The movement of the waters made thousands of sparks, silver and gold, at the same time. My retinas ached slightly in this brightness, unheard of on all other mornings. It seemed that all the night stars had forgotten to follow the blackness of the night and had fallen overboard, and were now drowning in their own intense, seething glow of the sun-warmed morning broth. I would be entertained for a long time in this landscape, but I had consulted my watch, there was little time left for my bus to pass. Besides, it was Friday, the day of the cargo flight in the morning, I couldn't be late. I left the parapet and approached the two, who were still busy preparing the powder with distilled water. The stranger noticed my presence.

"Everything is ready," he said.

There were papers on the floor. The double dose was already in the syringe, but he still made sure there weren't any air bubbles.

"I don't have much time," I said.

"Now it will be quick", said Dionysus, showing a cold smile. He then pressed the muscle of his arm with the palm of his hand, for the strange friend to introduce that needle into the startled vein. He did this with closed lips, keeping them thus until the end of the application; then it was to become of the stranger, who did the same, however, using the pressure of Dionysus' hands on his partner's arm.

Do not. It definitely couldn't be like that, it wasn't like that because the world wasn't just that, I saw the sun shining on the sea. I saw seagulls fly over the fishing boats returning to the beach. And when the nights were moonlit, white, passionate, I helped pull the trawlers with the old fishermen on the beach, winning tasty fish for my dinner. Yes, of course, I also tried cork cachaça to remove the salty taste from my tongue parched by the saline wind. Thus, it also took the cold off the legs submerged in the icy mantle of the night sea. Moreover, in that effort of bodies pulling the mesh under the moonlight, I also felt like them, I felt more like a human person, not afraid to dream every moment of my simple and intelligent life. That alone was enough for me; plus I had my job at the airport, whose service allowed me long breaks from fishing. It was at this time, incidentally, that I was lucky enough to meet some famous writers. Your books gave me courage for human adventures and a lot of will to live! Maybe one day I'll become a writer too! Yes, I would travel alone through the omnipresent time of the human soul and convey my friendship to lonely readers! Wow, that was really fascinating. I felt happy.

Now the two were, as they wanted. I don't know if it was the right thing to do. The stranger put the bottle of water and the disposable syringe back in the bag. Dionysus was waiting for us by the door. He looked out of this world, and the movement of his body gesture seemed relaxed in a certain cadence, recharged with more vigorous energy.

"All right?" He asked, seeing me watching him with wistful curiosity.

"Okay," I replied, lifting the door the same way I had opened it without making a sound. We return to the stairs. I fitted the latch to the ring and secured the padlock.

"You are late?" Dionísio wanted to know, going down first.

"Don't speak loudly," I whispered.

"I forgot," he whispered, too.

We descended the five floors in silence. I followed behind, following the circular staircase that seemed to have no end.

In front of the building, I already felt better. The smell of leaves and the song of morning birds were still present in my senses.

"Thank you," Dionísio said, raising his thumb in thanks. I didn't say anything beyond the gesture of looking at him in friendship. Even though I don't see him frequently, I even thought he was working or had moved to another neighborhood. Anyway, I was the one busy, traveling, being away for a long time. The two then walked down the deserted street while I remained leaning against the gate, looking at the ground, perhaps still trying to ask myself what had just happened.

We will see…

Just as I opened the bedroom window, yawning, they passed my window. One of them, recognizing me at a glance, waved, asking me to come down for a moment. It was him, Dionysus, one of my childhood friends. Without drinking my coffee, I set aside a few coins for the bus ticket, going down before the usual time. Well, as soon as I left the building's entrance, they came to me.

"Listen, Dan, I need your help, only you can break our problem", Dionysus had said with a worried look.

"To help?"

"Can you lend us the terrace?"

"I didn't understand."

"We need a peak."

For a few seconds, I didn't believe it, not knowing what to think or say. I was taken surprised, the request hit my newly awakened senses, I hadn't even had coffee.

"I don't know if I should do this, Dionysus", he said, still surprised, despite knowing that he was involved with drugs.

"It's windy on the shore," said the strange fellow with the bag in his hand.

"It'll be quick, no one will know", added Dionysus, right after.

"I'm going to take the bus", I informed him, looking at the clock, justifying my appointment.

"It's too early; the sun hasn't even risen yet!"

"I'm going to the airport."

"Are you going to travel?"

"No, I work in aviation, I'm a freight forwarder."

"What time does the bus leave?" Dionysus asked, looking toward the curved waterfront.

"In an hour," I replied naively.

"Plenty of time," he said, perking up.

"I don't know..." I hesitated.

"Come on, buddy, break this branch, I'm in the fissure, we won't be long, believe me!"

I was still undecided. I didn't do drugs, but I loved the sound of Jimi Hendrix's electric guitar! Moreover, I got goosebumps listening to Joe Cocker's husky voice! What about the poetic ballads of John Lennon, Bob Dylan? The jazz, the blue? Simply, all of them, drugs or no drugs (that was the least of it), were just too much! They conveyed the truth of our time directly, bluntly! The words came like stones down a hill! It was the stone, the speed, the image, the movement! This musical behavior was not maddening madness! It was art, a truth, a cultural rebellion!

"So, man, the terrace," he insisted.

"Okay," I said, afraid I'd regret it later.

"It was so worth it, buddy."

"No screaming, no scandal, I don't feel like playing anyone's lawyer and executioner, I already have too many problems to worry about in this life, now that's all that's missing: letting two crazy people get high on my terrace!"

The two looked at each other with a questioning expression, perhaps not understanding a single word of what I had just said. In fact, I didn't even understand.

"Let's be quiet, we won't make any noise," said Dionysus's friend, with a brief smile.

Well, that's how it happened. Now they are gone. They went around the curve of the beach, where the sea of Guanabara had changed with the brightness of the morning sun. I could hear ripples gently lapping against the oil-stained rocks, mixing the smells with the sea salt. I consulted my watch. It was at that moment, by the way, that the bus made the curve by the sea.

"Come on, one more day," I muttered sullenly, regretting the fast.

I crossed the street calmly, waited for the bus to arrive. Stopped. I took the stairs in one quick jump. In the same way, I passed the roulette wheel, handing the change to the changer, and then sat in front, almost next to the driver. The bus was empty, always with half a dozen passengers going to the service at that time. I opened the window and the cool morning air hit my face in a strong rush. I drew air into my lungs with a long sigh. *"Ah, never mind, forget this drug for good",* I thought looking out the window.

The bus had resumed the road, the journey. I watched the roofs of the houses, the sky going on over the vast infinity, revealing the great day that would be today. *"Yes, it will be a fine day,"* I said to myself.

"What did you say?" Asked the driver next to me, peeking at me slightly.

"Nothing, nothing at all". I replied, a little surprised to have muttered my thoughts with such impetus.

He looked at me again, not understanding what I had said to him about the engine noise.

"I said it's going to be a beautiful day!"

The driver looked at the sky through the windshield to check.

"Ah yes, young man, today will be a beautiful day, looks like you will like it!"

He shifted gears and went back to peering at the sky as he continued to drive, keeping a sharp eye on the road.

"Yes, that's right, you're absolutely right," he continued, "and by the way, many beaches, believe me, lots of cold beer, yeah, man, that's wonderful. Definitely a tan woman, each hotter than the last, we even lost our politeness, the passenger at the stop is attacking us on the corner, calling us a son of a bitch."

He spoke without taking his eyes off the road. I just smiled in agreement. And it continued.

"My São Cristóvão knows that. He knows I'm not serious, he knows how things are, the eyes don't obey, they get lost in the beauty of these women, do you understand me?"

I smiled, agreeing, now finding him funnier, he seemed excited, excited, this morning, he kept his eyes on the road, sometimes he looked at me briefly, asking:

"But it's not true?"

"Yes, that's true," he replied, smiling.

"Damn, this is the best of paradises. Saint Christopher knows this; I'll have to be born again. Yeah, man, I wasn't born into a rich family, with my ass facing the moon. The life of the poor is no joke; he knows that, I ate the bread that the devil kneaded. I cannot leave this Celestial Paradise, here there are only good women, cold beer, lots of sun, I don't know up there!"

I laugh in agreement.

"But isn't it true? Who guarantees us? Look at the sea, what beauty, what an extraordinary paradise we have here!"

Infecting me with animosity, also not knowing what to say, now I only had time to show my admiring smile followed by repeated nods, agreeing with everything he said offhand.

"But it's not true?"

"Yes it's true."

"And to know, with people who complain about life, who waste time with drugs, with crimes, with fights… How could something like that happen?"

He shifted gears, changed his voice, becoming deeper, plaintive.

"Of course, I should have known, I should also have come in shorts, open sandals. Without those ridiculous socks, which only make your feet sweat, bringing more foot odor. Of course, also coming with a silk shirt, that cold, soft one, after all I may not be rich, but I have refined taste. No doubt, it's going to be a very hot day,

I've seen it all, a lot of wing stink with the smell of sour onion, displeasure, you don't even want to ride a crowded bus at rush hour. My eggs cook, sometimes I feel like, I'm sitting on the stove, my balls are frying, my hemorrhoid starts to hurt. It feels like the folds are going to burst, and when the time comes, damn it, my throat is already dry, thirsty, the sweat on my body sticky, what the fuck..."

Then he switched gears and continued:

"And at that time, where's the cold draft beer, where's the dip in the sea, where's the hot chicks? This is horrible, very horrible, young man, believe me! On second thought, I believe it will not be a beautiful day, young man, I believe you deceived me..."

I didn't know whether to laugh or cry anymore...

"But isn't it true? It's going to be another hard day, very hot, I've seen everything, man, it'll be hell!" He kept saying. And before crossing the Galeão Bridge[10], when I was already on my feet, waiting to get off the bus, he said goodbye with a brief wave and smile, concluding:

"Okay, don't get discouraged. Tomorrow, God willing, we'll still get along. Please remember what I said, you are young; you'll have more time than me, so make the most of it, do it for me! At least I will feel a little better,

---

[10] The correct name is Prefeito Mendes de Moraes Bridge; it was the first road route built to connect Ilha do Governador to Ilha do Fundão and the mainland.

knowing that I opened the eyes of those who can still enjoy the life that God lent us!"

IGNORANCE OF THE WORD SKIFF

After the aircraft slowly circulated outside the runway, support teams arrived to carry out maintenance tasks and change the flight attendant, in addition to the generating plant car, the passenger bus and other transport vehicles for general supervision.

I had arrived driving a Kombi. I had to remove the documents that accompanied the cargo on that flight. Likewise, I parked near the first based on, already opened by the team of porters who pulled the boards close to the based on. As I approached the first one, I felt the icy breath coming from within. I took the metal box and took out the documents. They were also ice-cold. I opened one of the envelopes, stepping away from the handling. I went back to the Kombi. In the same way, I closed the door and raised the window to reduce the noise of the turbine. I consulted the weight guide. Only, 2800 kilos at first base and almost that at second. That was good. This meant more time in our favor, providing better conditions to board the next flight. I then went through the cargo manifests to make sure there were no perishable cargoes, reviewing them one by one when, at that point, I became aware of an urgent shipment. The word was typed and underlined in red, which meant more attention than the rest. I tried opening the document to see what it was about, but there were too many staples, making it difficult to extract the attachments. So, I looked at the first sheet, although the description on the cover didn't help one bit, except I knew the packaging must have been wood as it weighed 200 pounds. At this point, I looked out the window, to see if there was anything like that, but no, so far, only cardboard boxes, tied packages and a few burlap bags were coming out. While watching the movement, Fabiano, a colleague on duty, got into the car carrying a bottle of mineral water.

"Want a drink?" He asked, holding out the vial.

"No, thank you."

"What a hot day," he commented, tipping the bottle, informing that the ice on the wings had already melted, and there was no longer any refrigeration.

I was still looking at the loading plank with an air of concern.

"Some problem?"

"Do you know what coffin means?" I asked, rereading this word on the document clutched in my hands.

"Skiff," he repeated the word, thinking, vaguely…

I kept looking at the board.

"What's the weight of this..., what's the name of the thing again?"

"Skiff. It weighs 90 kilos."

"Wooden box," she said, placing the empty bottle beside the seat.

"Weird name," I commented, rereading the word again.

"Isn't that some water ski equipment? The name is almost similar."

"No. That kind of thing doesn't come with that description of urgency."

He appreciated the document in my hands.

"Why don't you open the attachments?"

"I'll wait, there are many staples, I don't want to pierce my fingers."

Did not take too long. Stunned, we saw a funeral coffin coming out of the based on.

"Skiff, just look at how much ignorance we have left poor mortals", said Fabiano without taking his eyes off the coffin.

When starting the engine, he got out of the car and went to meet another plane approaching at the head of the runway. I maneuvered the Kombi so that the side door was side by side with the board.

"Let's put the coffin here", I shouted to the team leader, using the strange word for the first time.

They quickly handled the coffin, arranging it on the floor of the Kombi. With the doors closed, I made a return behind the aircraft and took the yellow line of vehicles, entering the normal internal traffic lane, following the path to the position depot, about five kilometers from there.

During the trip, I thought about the skiff. Now the word wasn't just an unfamiliar word; in fact, more than the meaning of being a funeral urn, it was the meaning of our destiny. Yes, we fear death because we know nothing about it. It made me more ignorant for not knowing the meaning of that either; so, what was left for me to conclude was the certainty that we are not sure of anything, except that one day we all end up like this! Ah, but I had a lot of faith in my heart. No, the faith of seeking only the relief of our errors, our faults, in short, of obtaining only absolution. This for thinking about what we could still find after death. My faith was in the simple reason, naked and raw: just to live as long as one can live because, in fact, people do not come into the world just with the natural exercise of preparing for death; but above all to get to know each other. As long as there is life in our being, only life palpitates! This time is short, you see. Only the elderly, of advanced age, know this better than anyone else does. You always think about it when you see life ending, so there is more clarity when you are closer to death. Yes, I thought of all that now, it's true, all for the coffin that was back there. I didn't know who he was or how he died and what he would have done while he lived. Did it matter now? It was just a body. It was only a corpse lying in a box back there. Death had taken what he had lived, possibly not even he himself knew about its existence anymore. In that case, only those who know death, from the outside, that is, from the side of those who have already departed, would perhaps know much more than you and me. Therefore, I couldn't answer for myself anyway. It's useless to think about death while you're alive…

When I arrived at the depot, there was already a hearse waiting; soon, undertakers moved the coffin. I stood at the hangar door watching the car drive away, taking death far from me, at least at this time.

"Dan Paz", shouted the boss from inside the hangar, "stop thinking about an easy life, let's go to work!"

"I wasn't thinking about life," I said, returning to the hangar, "I was thinking about death, boss."

"In death? So much the worse, my boy, so much the worse", he said, as he looked at a load sheet he had in his hands, already showing it to me as he said:

We have a lot to do, look what awaits you here: four pallets[11] from freighter 265; therefore, save life insurance for later, now there is no time to think about it!"

---

[11] Pallet: frame made up of a metal sheet, on which the load is stacked in a pyramid shape, often used in loading cargo planes.

"I was just thinking about death when I saw the skiff," I said, showing the copy of the document signed by the undertaker.

"Skiff? What the hell is that?"

"Oh boss, I thought you knew, everyone knows what it is. It's a funeral coffin", I replied, showing my knowledge of the word.

"Oh, frankly, Dan," he said after glancing briefly at the document in my hands. "We have an eternity to think about death when we die! Believe me; let death take care of the dead while life takes care of the living! And look," he said, showing the south side of the hangar. "That batch still needs to be checked for tomorrow's shipment".

Moreover, turning quickly towards the north sector, he called out to the dispatcher who was running past in the distance, giving him a shout in an unnerved voice that stopped him immediately.

"Tell Luiz Guerra to come soon, flight 265 has already started to board!"

Then he turned to me.

"Are you still here, Dan? That's what happens when you think about death: you always end up forgetting about life!"

THE TREASURE DISPATCHER

From what I could testify, he knew how to do the best job in special transport. Either on merit or competence, or on the sole responsibility of his personal character, he was chosen to supervise the transport of the most valuable precious stones in the jewelry market. Evidently, it was the strange trade in emeralds, diamonds, rubies, turquoises, sapphires and a lot of gold going in ingots a span long, weighing approximately three and a half kilos. From this varied treasure, we could imagine that these precious stones would be meticulously polished by the skillful hands of magnificent jewelers, transforming them into beautiful jewels of pure grade or carat. However, although this did not happen immediately, that is, for the final shipment, the goods previously passed through the handling screen that preceded the air shipment. First, it went through a thorough check of the invoices with their respective corresponding volumes. Then the boxes still had to be completely sealed with thin nails, enameled wax, in addition to reinforcing stainless-steel strips around each numbered package, ending the examination with a red seal from jeweler suppliers. So, the second phase of this movement was to pack all this fortune in burlap sacks, which were immediately sewn with wire and numbered lead seal over the knot of the metal crosspieces. Finally, it was ready for the position to be loaded.

Well, with all this planned with all the logistical precautions, none of it would still be secure enough to prevent theft. Mysteriously, this still happened during the journey of the precious cargo, from the warehouse to the route of the aircraft. Nothing was known exactly where and when the sinister thefts took place. Whole lots disappeared as if by magic in front of us all. For insurers, the millionaire figure in losses was enormous. Not to mention the loss of jewelry customers.

From what later became known, dispatcher Moura had been chosen for this mission. He was to monitor future shipments of gems from the hangar as they moved across the runway. He had to be the last passenger on board and the first one out, whatever it was, he couldn't take his eyes off the treasure as long as the aircraft remained on the ground. Obviously, it wasn't just merit or competence. He was the person indicated by his obsessive desire to see the position shipped without error, whether precious or common cargo, nothing could go wrong with his shipments that was his operating strength.

Antônio Moura became a legend. Incredibly, it shipped over 500 tons of domestic cargo annually without using freighter flights. Thus, he gained a lot of prestige. International dispatchers admired him for not accumulating national cargo in the Galeão hangars, so that the holds of cargo flights to Viracopos would have more space for exclusive international flights without having to share spaces with national cargo. In addition, he had the extraordinary feat of knowing how to deal with the auxiliary team integrated in the handling of cargo. This included hangar and runway loaders, respectively. He went from trucks to surfboards (vice versa). This was not an easy task for a forwarding agent to carry out with an outsourced support service, as indigestible men participated in this type of work, including bandits infiltrated by the organized crime mafia. However, the professional respect was mutual. The camaraderie was frequent, especially when there was another supportive hand added in handling understaffed teams. By the way, not at all appreciated by the predecessor dispatchers. The latter; for example, had been removed from his duties due to serious human negligence, although — if we learned later — it was the work of some members of the group improvising in last-minute shipments.

Obviously, this implied liability risks for third parties in effecting immediate shipment. Based on the reasons analyzed, the dispatcher had exceeded the superhuman physical limit, forcing the shippers to move a lot of cargo in a very short period. Pressure on auxiliary support teams became intense. Fortunately, so a trusted team leader told me, it was just as a new employee appeared in that last minute of loading the load. That provided a timely maneuver: revenge on the arrogant dispatcher, urgently. So, the new loader was sign by a teammate to stay in the hold, with the task of organizing the volumes dumped quickly from the plank to the hold mouth.

"Yes, it was very lucky," he said, explaining that fateful day. "After all, let's face it, all our efforts were redoubled in the same proportion as our dissatisfaction, until the appearance of the novice in cargo handling came to change things. Yeah, man, we were exhausted. Our clothes were soaked with sweat in the 40-degree heat, believe me. This dispatcher ignored. He just wanted to shout, give orders. Nevertheless, in time, you see, the last volume was thrown in, and soon the cellar lid was locked. The engines had already accelerated as we tried to get away from the plane that was moving in front of the runway, ready to take off. Yeah, man, that was really lucky. We had to do this for the good of our union", he commented, with a sneaky look, always with that same malice typical of treacherous bandits, later adding with a cold smile:

"Yes, man, you had to check his expression, when they came to tell them that the rookie had been trapped in the hold. The man went white, paralyzed, as he saw the plane disappearing in the middle of the clouds. I even thought he was going to faint, such was the astonishment of knowing that one of our porters had been trapped in the based on to show the strength of our union..."

My God, I was talking about the treasure dispatcher, yes, look at the traps. I didn't realize. I was also inattentive. The rookie had been, trapped precisely in the hold of the flight that was following dispatcher Moura. Not that he was the reason. For him, by the way, it made no difference either. Whatever happened, even that wouldn't draw his attention.

As he descended from the aircraft, he was surprised to see the novice emerge from among the bundles. However, he couldn't take his attention away from the bags of gems taken from the board. The rookie, as far as he was concerned, recognizing the legendary treasure dispatcher, standing there before him, instantly jumped out of the cellar and ran towards him, screaming that those crazy motherfuckers had closed the cellar with him in it! Dispatcher Moura, under the turbines, although alarmed, but without paying attention to him (he couldn't take his eyes off the precious cargo), replied dryly that this was not his problem, that he should go and complain to his boss.

"I am two and a half hours away from the galleon, how can I complain?" insisted the porter.

At that same moment, still with the turbines on, a Kombi appeared bringing the track inspector from that base. The dispatcher would receive the special cargo. He approached his colleague Antônio Moura and, very close to his ear, shouted this bombastic comment:

"Wow, this time the treasure must be very valuable, I even brought a watchman in the basement, God help me!"

THE VOMIT SACK EPISODE

There was always a sordid airport story to hear or tell at those retired veteran mechanic's meetings. With a certain nostalgic magic, they always recalled the old days of commercial aviation in our country. One of those stories, incidentally, inadvisable, to be read by someone more scrupulous than my twenty-something years of life, was a story I heard from one of those legendary storytellers. For this reason, I already warn that this funny episode intended for those more accustomed readers with a working sense of humor. It is a sordid and vile story. Therefore, for those who are disgusted with everything, including a weak stomach, they won't say later that I didn't warn them.

Well, I was going into the maintenance hangar to wait for a poet friend. He was already in the process of publishing his first book, whose title, at least at the time, would suggest that it would actually be 'Flight of a Wingless Poem'. An allusion to the fact of living under planes, not inside them, flying. Surprisingly, I found myself facing this circle of veteran mechanics of the turboprop generation. Everyone gathered silently around the breakfast table, listening to an employee of the extinct Panair[12] narrate the story that occurred a few decades ago. Yes, that episode had circulated in several other airports in Brazil; perhaps in the world, as if it were a funny legend, but everyone at the time affirmed its veracity...

"Well then," said the veteran narrator, who, luckily for me, had barely begun to speak.

"Well, one day, the cleaning lady Zená got on Captain JP's plane to do the usual cleaning, despite not being part of the cleaning team on board; the fact, incidentally, that she caught the attention of the Commander when leaving the cockpit. Then he wanted to know if she was new to the job because if she were, he would need to give her some preliminary explanations. She replied that she wasn't very new to the service. She worked in the maintenance job, so she had some experience..."

"Yes, I understand that", he said, interrupting her, "what I want to know is if you are really one of the ship's cleaning people".

"Oh man, aircraft cleaning, I'm about new, yeah, sir", she replied, but adding that she could help on the

[12] Panair do Brasil S.A. was one of Brazil's pioneering airlines, headquartered in Rio de Janeiro, founded on October 22, 1929, by Ralph Ambrose O'Neill, one of the first five flying aces of the United States in World War I.

spur of the moment, as the misfortune of many cleaning women had happened on the same day.

"Anyway, you don't have to worry about misconduct (she meant embezzlement), as this service is the same everywhere."

Well, the commander took off his cap and smoothed the wispy white hair from his sun-reddened head as he thought of a better ruse. That didn't take two seconds, then he said again:

"Yes, yes, I know you do your job very well, but there is something I need to explain further as you are filling in for the other cleaning lady." Zená, all shy, already rolling the flannel between her fingers, marveling at been talking to a commander in uniform from head to toe, continued listening attentively. He asked her to pay attention to the paper bags...

"Yes, those that are useful for seasickness", confirmed the commander when he got a little closer to the ear to whisper, in an almost whispering tone, this request:

"Well, if you happen to find a bag..."and looked around, before continuing to say, "used bag; evidently, I want you to take it very carefully in my cabin without anyone noticing, okay?"

The cleaner, upon hearing the strange request, could only agree, saying yes, with a nod and wide eyes. He, noticing her astonishment, reassured her, explaining that he was just trying to make sure of the possibility, remote that it was, this there could be one passenger who was feeling sick during the journey.

"These are measures I decided to take after hearing malicious rumors about the peculiar way I fly. I don't know if you understand me, considering the growing and decreasing market of commercial aviation, bad tongues are always talking about people behind."

Zená understood while nodding her head in the affirmative. Afterward, she said it was true. There were bad people and talkers in this world. Despite this, she was informer that she would only find bags of candy wrappers, as, as far as she knew, during her flight, they was used only for that purpose, never with vomit.

"Even so," he said back, "even so, you can't be too careful. Many pilots are jealous of me. Yes, it's hard to believe that. I see in her eyes the surprise and doubt assailing her thoughts. However, true what I'm telling you. I am referring, of course, mainly to this whole generation of new pilots. They don't know how to fly a real plane. Not like this one, obviously. They are used to flying modern planes, full of useless clocks. I want to see them fly a turboprop, shit their pants, you know?"

Well, the cleaner Zená was impressed. In fact, nobody would believe it, not even the cleaners on board, especially Dolores, who had been absent because she was in pain in the rooms. She would be horrified to know that. Well then, the commandant JP, now adjusting his cap on his head, arranging his tie better, ended up saying that he would go back to his cabin. Although he still had time to warn her not to forget this detail: take the seat number too; of course, that was in case he found the inconvenience. However, that was the only way he could consult the passenger list, preventing him from traveling on his plane the next time.. Upon hearing this, the cleaner widened her eyes again, until the flannel fell from her hands.

Well, half an hour later, the cleaning lady found the bag. She would feel a chill as soon as she laid eyes on him. She was after all sure she wouldn't find such a thing on her plane. Just as there were those who said, he was a crazy, dirty commander, there were those who said he was the best pilot in the company. Yes, that's right. There were those who said he landed his plane like a feather, gliding down the runway without any trepidation. That's why she had been very hesitant about picking up the paper bag to show it in the cabin. The poor captain had to do everything possible and impossible not to shake the plane so that no one would get sick; now, as if all the sacrifice in vain wasn't enough, this bag full of vomit appeared. Well, orders are orders, what could she do? Even more so, because it was a commander's orders; therefore, she had plenty of reason for the order to be carried out, no matter how strange it was. Thinking like this, without further hesitation, he decided to go to the cabin with the bag hanging from his fingertips. Although she told herself, perhaps to gain more courage, that this could only be the work of some envious pilot posing as a false infiltrator, as he had rightly warned. Well, when she entered the cabin and the captain noticed the bag suspended in her fingers, she immediately rose from her seat, while saying:

"I can't believe they got an asshole to puke on my plane!"

The cleaning lady, scared, immediately tried to say that it hadn't been her. At the same time, timidly, she tried to resolve the situation, following him down the hall with the bag still hanging from her fingertips, saying:

"Commander, you don't need to be alarmed just because of that, I'm already throwing this crap in the trash and nobody will know!"

He seemed not to care what she said, taking off and replacing his cap several times in a row, with her continuing to say:

"Commander, don't worry, I'm going to put this filth in the garbage can, nobody will find out". Then, suddenly, he grabbed her by the arm to stop her, telling her to wait, that someone might see her with that thing in her hands…

He didn't seem to hear her. He continued to say:

He didn't seem to hear her. He continued to say:

"They are everywhere watching my movements. Yes, they want to end my career! No, no, ma'am, if you'll excuse me, hand over the bag, let me see," he said, taking it with a sudden devilish smile.

"Ah! It's those yellowish vomits, but why you didn't tell me before, I can't resist these," he said with startled eyes, with a macabre smile revealed in his teeth...

Suddenly, frighteningly, then, he emptied the entire contents of the bag down his throat, then pulled the white handkerchief from his pocket to wipe the corner of his lips discreetly, despite the slight burp that had escaped his lips...

My God, the cleaning lady, horrified, even witnessed the commander crush the bag, making a little ball of paper while he rubbed his stomach with another hand, saying these words in a more relieved tone:

"There, ma'am, now, yes, no one will believe what they just watched. It's preferable that way, I don't know if you understand me. In the end, the sacrifice is worth it. I'm sorry, but in her time, the lady would vent, tell this secret, saying that she found this vomit on my plane, and therefore, doing what I did now, nobody will believe you."

He raised the ball of paper to his lips to add:

"Although these yellowish vomits, I must confess, are delicious indeed."

Well then, the cleaning lady Zená, poor thing, ran away, and he ran after her, trying to reach her to clarify things better, still telling her, shouting:

"Wait, don't run like that, you might fall, roll down the stairs, wait, you didn't tell me seat number!"

Later, the head of maintenance found Zená all huddled in the corner of the room. With great cost, he found out what had happened. So, he explained to Zená that the commander put *guaraná*[13] with cracker crumbs in the nausea bag, shook it, and then left it on any armchair, always telling an absurd or tragic story as a starter.

Zená was furious for almost a week. She flatly refused to clean any aircraft. Let him go to the Pope's plane! Cursing all shameless crazy commanders! Afterward, she began to relate this story to her friends amid general laughter. Well, she ended up gaining prominence in meetings with stories and anecdotes, but swearing that everything was true.

Well, I justify, but I warned you: it was a funny and sordid story, very sordid, don't blame me for that, I'm a mere witness, I only told you this because I'm a mere writer, sorry.

---

[13] Guarana is a vine originating in the Amazon, whose fruit is industrially produced in sweetened soft drinks.

THE LONE SWIMMER

When swimming miles out to sea, the coast almost disappears behind the blue projections of the ocean, gradually producing, with each stroke, a certain lonely emotion of a maritime adventurer. Yes, a maritime adventure with only experienced swimmers. For this, the swimmer needs to be sure of his organic capacity and muscular strength, above all to enjoy full health and self-confidence. Without that performance, going too far is suicide. It would be necessary to transport oneself within oneself because it is in this effort that all the strength and courage stored in the depths of the soul reside. It is the state of survival, which the suicide has no such purpose.

That's precisely what I felt while swimming on the high seas. It would go far, as far as the ocean could swim, to reach my goal. Moreover, when I stopped my strokes and floated watching the sky, feeling my whole body immersed in the body of the sea, my existence mixed up with these two chemical amplitudes shape part of my being. In the distance, I saw the coast almost disappear. Then he returned slowly, slowly. Breaststroke revitalized me when I resorted to synchronized breathing. It rescued the lightness of already heavy limbs, but without failing to overcome the pull of the most revolting waves on the surface. I pushed my body further and further to the edge, until I came out of the sea like Neptune out of an ocean drunk with foam and salt.

Before returning to the hotel, I always stopped by Cabral's bar. There, I sat at the table overlooking the sea while I replenished my energy; then I chatted with the waiter, Jaime Romano, whom I maintained a deep friendship and admiration for many years. However, as I was saying, at that time, with a full stomach, the spirit of Neptune had left my body more than an hour and a half ago, while I was already finishing my meal.

"What did you think of Badejo[14]?" The old friend wanted to know.

"Great, the potatoes too."

"Since you didn't arrive, I moved the brazier away."

"I wasted a lot of time floating."

---

[14] Whiting (Badejo) is a species of marine fish common in parts of the northeastern Atlantic Ocean along the western coasts of Europe and the North Sea.

"It's been a long way, so..." He said, already transferring the plates and the jug of juice to the table, and sat down next to me.

"Better than yesterday," I informed.

"That's great," he smiled.

"And your day?"

"Well, Monday is always a quiet day around here."

"Now much more," I commented, referring to the end of the high season, when tourism decreased and the price of gastronomy as well.

"It's our, become to get some rest."

"Yes," I sighed.

"Would you like a beer?"

"Tomorrow," I replied.

"Swimming is good."

I looked at him, intrigued. I decided to take a risk.

"Tomorrow I'm going to swim to Mantarraya[15]," I informed.

"Careful, corals are treacherous," he said gravely.

"I'll access it from the beachside, don't worry."

The expression on his face suddenly changed. Perhaps I would discover the mystery, I thought.

---

[15] Mantarraya, also known as 'manta ray', 'manta', 'maroma', 'sea bat', 'devil fish', 'devil ray', is a cartilaginous, pelagic, flattened, oceanic fish whose species also takes the name of the island.

"Sometimes I miss the almost native young man who used to swim in this region," he said, as he looked towards Mantarraya Island in the distance.

. Once again, our conversation repeated itself. I followed his distant gaze, my heart racing, sensing the delicate situation.

"What happened to him? Died?" I asked, trying to be natural.

"No," he replied, become to me, looking serious as well.

"He still lives in this region," he added.

"Then what is the reason for longing?"

"He swam like that, like you. It's been a long time, almost 30 years. On that occasion, he won the Crossing of Guanabara medal. The man even swam well."

To my despair, someone seemed to approach the tables, but soon followed. Excellent. Our conversation continued.

"Does he not practice anymore?"

"He broke his arms there," he continued, looking out over the island with an expression of sudden sadness.

Now, with luck, I felt that this time I couldn't go wrong again, I just needed to break the spell.

"Was it surfing?" I ventured to ask another way, although he had answered these questions before.

He smiled slyly, but still, yes, with sadness in his eyes. I realized that I had made another mistake, that the charm would never dissipate, in short, the same escape as always.

"You won't believe it, he said, recovering, a sting-ray jumped on him, imagine, mantarraya, which one, with the long tail, looked like the black and white devil! You're not from Botafogo[16], are you? Well, it doesn't matter. The idiot was startled to see her flying over him. Then, in desperation, he changed the course of his blows, slamming into the rocks. A perfect idiot, as you can see."

"How did you manage to escape?"

"Luck, I don't know, maybe a miracle."

The waiter, now lowering his eyes as if he had gone back to that time, explained that the two fishermen watched the moment of disaster. Then he explained that one of them climbed the rock with his cast net and a rope hook. Managed to hoist him up in the intervals of the biggest waves, soon pulling him over the rocks. He also explained that they thought he had already died he was all bloodied so that it would really be a miracle to stay alive. After all, he wasn't even moving; even so, they accommodated the body in the canoe and soon rowed towards the village of Colonia Açores; from there he was taken by ambulance to the capital…

---

[16] Botafogo Futebol e Regatas is a Brazilian multi-sport association, based in the neighborhood of the same name, in the city of Rio de Janeiro.

He stopped talking. I was still impressed. I kept thinking about everything he had just said to me. Not because of the story, after all I had already heard the same story more than once. Yes, a constant repetition because when I met him, I was impressed to learn from his partner (both owners of Cabral), that the young man who had drowned on the island of Mantarraya, was nothing more than the waiter himself. He had developed a second personality. Something like an enchantment, a spell. This is because he did not admit to being a victim of drowning, as reported by the fishermen. Furthermore, they claimed not to have seen the Manta Ray. Consequently, this ended up raising doubts about the veracity of the report. Upon learning of this, the waiter began to call his rescuers (eyewitness) lying fishermen! Evidently, the fact made the news, after all he was a well-known long-distance swimmer. Anyway, time has passed in these 30 years. Everything was forgotten. However, something changed in his personality. He denied his youth as a swimmer. It was as if, remembering his own past, he was now experiencing something in the third person. So, I found it very strange that he acted that way, maybe it was a trauma. Yes, it was something deeper, psychological, something very difficult to understand.

Returning to the subject, I continued our conversation.

"Well," I said, thinking, "at least he made it through. It could have been worse."

"Undoubtedly," he agreed, "coral encrusted in rocks cuts like shards of glass or razors!"

Again, we were silent, admiring the sea. The fishing boats had advanced to the coast. They were heading for the pier, after crossing the cliff at the point, where the beach cove began. The day was ending. I thought about my vacation ending too. However, there was still the week to go; the routine would start all over again. It would be harder to relax and swim when I got back to work. Not that it was the reason, not exactly, but he was excited about long-distance swimming in the open water. It was the solitary freedom of swimming with no strings attached, just training without worrying about the timer.

The conversation with the waiter friend had piqued my curiosity, so I returned to the subject. I decided to ask what should have happened to that stingray; after all, it jumped in that risky way.

"Usually, they flee from any human approach," he said looking at me sincerely, probably because he understood that I believed him and not those fishermen, in fact, ignorant about the knowledge of maritime life, only fishing life.

"So what made her jump?"

"Mating, that was it, the male wanting to play tricks on the female. Anyway, how do you know if, nowadays, pollution is messing with your secular instincts, too?"

"I think it would scare me just as much," I said, thinking seriously.

"Anyone would be scared by that creature with open fins jumping over it. Anyway, it was precipitation for him to have swum towards the rocks."

"I think I would resort to the stones, too."

He looked at me puzzled.

"Serious?"

"Yes," I stated, remembering a similar fact.

"I once confused a dolphin's fin with a shark's fin. My heart raced, I panicked. I swam swiftly towards the shore, thinking only of escaping!"

"Exactly, you get the gist of it, not like those bragging swimmers out there! Right here," he said to me, now, turning towards the bar, altering his voice, giving the impression that from inside the bar his partner could hear him better, so he continued to say:

"Right here, you won't believe it, right here we find swimmers of that nature: they don't know how to swim and that's why they think everyone drowns!"

"He doesn't think that about you."

"He doesn't believe she did it!"

"Do you really think so?"

"Well, what does it matter now? Thirty years have passed! Besides, no one believed this story!"

"Okay, that's because none of them have seen a stingray jump over you while you're swimming."

"Even if it wasn't the reason for mating, what makes a stingray jump like that? Yes, I know, the male is not afraid of the swimmer, but they run away because they prefer not to draw anyone's attention! Even so, who's to say she didn't run away because she couldn't care less about the presence of humans? Now, just because a rooster rolls his neck and sticks out his chest when it's time to do the job, that doesn't mean that all roosters should always act the same every time they want to fuck! Wouldn't you agree with me? That happens with stingrays too!"

"I've never seen a rooster act otherwise," I replied, finding the comparison amusing.

"Neither do I," he said seriously, "but who knows what shouldn't happen in the dead of night in the chicken coop? Let the rooster live at night!"

I laughed.

"But it's true!" He continued explaining in earnest. "These are the new times! I noticed this, really, because the other day, hey, I was coming home from work and didn't I suddenly see a dog on top of a plastic doll? Yes, the bastard had his tongue out, imagine, the bastard wanted to stick the pangolin[17] in the doll, have you ever seen anything like that? So is! A dog that does this, believe me, is under the manic influence of our depraved society. Listen to what I tell you because in his right

---

[17] Softer slang expression to, not say 'fuck' explicitly.

mind, I mean, in his natural state as a normal dog, he would certainly go after a bitch without ever thinking of picking up a plastic doll! That's why I insist, young man, today's animals are, in fact, changing about the natural behavior of the thing, believe me!"

"It's not common", I said, between laughs, "but there can be, yes, exceptional cases…"

"Exceptional? I already see it as a genetic alteration, I don't know, something in the DNA!"

"It's possible?"

"No doubt! Take it in the psychological sense of it, if that's what you mean. I don't even want to discuss changes in the evolution of species, I don't know why, from that standpoint, we are already entering the worrying subject of the sudden changes that occur on the planet…"

"Yes, I know," I agreed, more seriously. "For example, the phenomenon of pollution as a cause of biochemical alteration factors that interact negatively with the behavior of species."

"Well, don't you see? We enter the most intrinsic sense of the psychological behavior of the species!"

Moreover, as if looking for another way to express himself, he added:

"Listen to this. If you take a couple of penguins out of their habitat, there will certainly be a change in the emotional behavior of that species that this happens, even with any type of animal that enters captivity. Privately, the penguin has a unique and direct characteristic of revealing his mating intentions: he simply deposits a stone at the female's feet, isn't it true? Of course, if she agrees with the fertilization proposal. The rest is, known how everything happens, not to mention that this ritual is repeated with several back and forth, until the female chooses the stone that awakens the proposed desire with the characteristic of the shape of the egg. In other words, it works like a good song. So, man, see how much psychology of love happens between these two before intercourse!"

"What does this have to do with habitat change? As a rule, these emotional changes arise with many species brought into captivity, no matter how similar the new home looks, they initially cause changes, but then they get used to it!"

"That's what you think," replied the waiter, with an expression of astonishment. "In the case of the penguin, for example, it entirely changes the symbolic expression of the stone!"

"Like this?"

"Okay, I know I don't have scientific proof of what I'm going to tell you. However, I witnessed with my own eyes the infuriating way in which a female refused the stone in the very first moment the male made a move to pick it up. She simply gave him a neurasthenic scolding as if to say: 'don't even think about such a thing', while the male, anxiously trying to explain himself, going after her, said: 'but, darling, we need to fertilize', while, she, seeming to retort, said: 'here in this gated community with all the same stones, but don't even think about that'!"

"Do you want to drive me crazy or do you want to kill me with laughter," I said, laughing again.

"I'm serious; things have been very sinister lately!"

He stopped talking. I took advantage of getting up from the table.

"So you really don't have a beer?" He asked getting up too.

"Tomorrow, after the island," I replied, still laughing.

He got serious all of a sudden.

"Don't worry, everything will be fine."

"Okay, in that case I'll prepare another Badejo, then I'll tell you why the swimmer of 30 years ago didn't want to swim anymore."

I stopped, perplexed. Suddenly, I had noticed his gaze! By Neptune, he knew who the lone swimmer he had been talking about was, he knew himself in the third person!"

Jaime Romano was 82 years old when he died. His mortuary countenance still maintained a proud personality, his white hair disheveled, and his old face still tanned by the sun; that's because, in life, when very young, he was diagnosed with Asperger's syndrome; however, the son of aquatic sportsmen, he became state champion in long-distance swimming, having won several events at Travels Guanabara. In 1954, he traveled to England and, two years later, aged just 18; he crossed the English Channel literally alone, that is, without telling anyone. Obviously, this has never, been proven. In 1957, he participated in the Commonwealth Trans Antarctic Expedition, the first to cross Antarctica; and in Patagonia, when he experimented with zoology and botany in the National Park Los Glaciares, under the Andes Mountains, and then traveled through the mountains of the vast regions of Fitz Roy and Cerro Torre. Upon returning to Brazil, he coached the younger generations of swimmers who would excel at the next Olympics. His life, however, changed radically after he was rescued by fishermen[JC1][JC2] *on the island of Mantarraya while swimming away from shore. Thereafter, he was never the same man, suffering further relapses of autism; so much so that, when speaking of his own past, he seemed to be speaking of someone apart from himself. He worked as a waiter and partner at Bar do Cabral, whose owner was the grandson of Mr. Lucio de Cabral; famous rower of that region, very friendly with his grandfather, the illustrious Dr. DJ Romano, great researcher at the Institute of Zoology, but that's another longer story…*

A DOOR OPENS

They had to call the director of the school into our classroom: the Artistic Education teacher had interrupted her explanation of how the technical course classes would be like, but had to go out the door, unexpectedly. I was stunned. From what she understood, she was explaining the proposal to hold classes that would awaken the student's sensitivity. A new critical view of the world through artistic creation, developing aesthetic perception among different schools of painting. The respective expressions of time. All this took less than ten minutes. There were a few unwelcome interruptions from disgruntled colleagues. When she left the room, everyone was still excited. The chatter of discontent was general. The director had to enter the room, then patiently place himself in front of the painting, until the chatter, slowly, become into a murmur. Before the clock even ticked another minute, everyone fell silent.

"Something went wrong?" The principal wanted to know, looking calmly at the class.

"We are not interested in Art classes," said one student who seemed to represent the entire class.

"I'm also here for another reason," said another student in the middle of the class.

"Yes, that's right," said another at the back of the room, where, behind him, high on the wall, there was a poster of a welder hanging from a steel scaffolding, probably photographed at the Rio de Janeiro shipyard.

"What is the use of this to our profession?" asked another.

The director chose a piece of chalk from the box and, in capital letters, wrote the word CULTURE. He deposited the chalk on the blackboard credenza and become to the class, wiping his hands. Then he said that teacher Ivone was at school to pass on the word he had written. Only one day a week, always on Fridays, in the last term; finally, it would not be a mandatory subject in the course program; but, at the same time, his classes could serve as an aid in the complementary scoring of the mandatory subjects.

The director chose a piece of chalk from the box and, in capital letters, wrote the word CULTURE. He deposited the chalk on the blackboard credenza and become to the class, wiping his hands. Then he said that teacher Ivone was at school to pass on the word he had written. Only one day a week, always on Fridays, in the last term; finally, it would not be a mandatory subject in the course program; but, at the same time, his classes could serve as an aid in the complementary scoring of the mandatory subjects.

The director, however, continued unabated, waiting for the hubbub and laughter to die down. Indeed, the class fell silent again and he continued his explanation.

"You are students from the Lins de Vasconcelos Technical School", he said, in a calm voice. "Therefore, you must understand that you are here exclusively to obtain professional technical training for mechanics, but that does not mean disregarding everything that you consider less important, does it? Leonardo da Vinci, for example, was a scientist who painted, wrote, researched and developed extensive projects based on the principles of mechanics! On the other hand, you know, they are famous paintings, the manuscripts too! However, what impresses most about this genius, not precisely the entrepreneurial spirit of the scientific research he developed? We can even say that he was the first scientist to diversify the project of several contemporary sciences, including anatomy."

"Excuse me, director." Interrupted the student who seemed to represent the class. "Everything is very fascinating, wonderful, no doubt. However, we don't have a lot of time; most of us spend our entire day working. We barely ate enough to come here to train ourselves in what we set out to study, but don't you think that, after all that, we still need to learn something that is not part of our exclusive program?"

There was another hubbub, this time with many raised voices.

"That's right," said someone from the back of the room, shyly agreeing with the director.

"This is not right because we pay for this professional improvement, which gives us the right to demand only what interests us from the specific course", replied another, still retorting.

The class got more excited. Everyone spoke simultaneously. In this hubbub of voices, the majority shared the opposite opinion: no one would have the obligation to supervise what does not suit them. The director, however, remained obstinate, having now raised his hand, questioning once more.

"What can I say to convince them to change? Your colleague", he said showing him briefly with a hand gesture, then continued to explain:

"Unfortunately, he fails to understand the dimension and importance of art from the perspective of his profession! If he had, for example, the miraculous opportunity to go back to Leonardo da Vinci's time and learn his art, two things could happen: either he would become a great scientist due to the high price of mechanics, or, in this case, more specifically the which I mean, just another mere screwdriver given the lack of interest in art!"

There was a fatal silence. The director went to the blackboard, took the eraser and passed it three, four times over the word he had written minutes before, and then returned to the room with a convincing look, concluded:

"Arts Education, as I said before, is not a review, but it helps with student performance. It will also serve as a complement if the student needs extra points in tests that he cannot take during the semester. That's good, a plus. Thus, everyone can advance to the next curricular segment, in addition to obtaining extra pedagogical knowledge about universal culture and art! Therefore, I leave you this option: the free option to choose what is most advantageous for you! Good night everyone and have a nice weekend!"

He quickly left the room, leaving forty-five students in silence.

There were only eight classes. Unfortunately, teacher Ivone resigned from the school. Certainly, because of the embarrassment created around her classes. The small number of students who remained in the classroom was regrettable. When Friday came, there were always half a dozen cats left. This caused deep frustration in the teacher, who with her head down sadly waited for most of the class to leave, and then started the class.

I was very upset when I learned of your resignation. He was learning about Modern Art, whose first artists, among other schools, were the Impressionist painters. The teacher had been scheduling classes with slides, showing us paintings by Monet, Renoir, and Matisse... so it would be expressionist painters. In the last class, we had a sample of slides about the work of Picasso, the most representative artist of our century. In fact, we were, I mean, only half a dozen cats, we were, very moved by so much beauty seen in those paintings. His classes simply relaxed us after hours of logical reasoning about calculations and equation formulas for testing light and heavy metals. All this, not counting the chemical elements of electromagnetic program in combustion engines. Therefore, it was necessary to develop calculations of mechanical capacity of heavy machines and variations of thermal engines, which I ended up bugging with all that shit, sending everything to hell!

I went to the secretary to lock the register.

"But right now, at the end of the semester?"

"That's right."

"Are you traveling, by any chance?"

"No sir."

The director entered the job, examining a letter he had in his hand.

"So why?" The secretary continued.

"Private reasons."

The director noticed something wrong and wanted to know what was going on.

"This student wants to withdraw enrollment," said the secretary, adjusting his glasses.

The director watched me, intrigued.

"Are you giving up?"

"I am."

He thought for a few seconds, looking me in the eyes.

"May I know why?"

For a moment, I almost answered what I had said to the secretary, but when I noticed him frankly and sincerely waiting for the answer, I decided to tell him the truth.

"I'm off to learn some of Leonardo da Vinci's art."

The headmaster's puzzled look immediately become to a delighted, satisfied smile.

"You mean you won't be tightening screws anymore?"

"No sir."

He immediately put his arm around my shoulder as he addressed the secretary.

"Mr. Alves, try to lock this young man's registration soon, an artist can't waste time when he decides!"

After leaving the Lins de Vasconcelos Technical School, returning by bus, I remembered teacher Ivone and the director's last words. Yep, he was a friend, and I was screw free. Now everything was present in my spirit, including my youth searching for new paths to tread, accumulating years and years of many memories about human relationships, from when I was younger and immature. I didn't regret anything, not even the mistakes I had committed and would perhaps still commit, while they, in one way or another, would also serve as life lessons, not repeat them. Therefore, as the bus approached the neighborhood, it was as if I were also approaching an invisible portal. Yes, a portal, a portal that opened to the future. I just needed to cross it, then I would start writing thanks to the initial incentive of artistic education, it was the discovery that palpitated in my heart!

FIM

https://twitter.com/home
https://juidson.blogspot.com
https://portal.uiclap.com

Livro impresso

Tipografias — ***Palatino LT. 12* — *Times New Roman 11/ 16/ 18***

www.ingramcontent.com/pod-product-compliance
Lightning Source LLC
LaVergne TN
LVHW010555160826
845677LV00013B/3137

* 9 7 9 8 3 7 4 9 5 3 2 9 9 *